S0-AQL-113

Usborne Illustrated Stories for Boys

Usborne Illustrated Stories for Boys

Edited by Lesley Sims and Louie Stowell
Designed by Tom Lalonde
Cover design by Zoë Wray
Cover illustration by Ian McNee

Contents

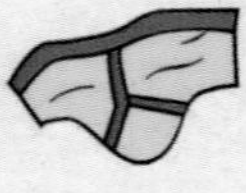

Sam Sardine had always wanted to be a sailor.

He was desperate to travel the Seven Seas and do battle with bloodthirsty pirates.

As soon as he was old enough, he joined Captain Winkle's ship as a cabin boy.

But Sam soon found that life on board ship wasn't as exciting as he'd thought.

He spent all day...

mopping the decks...

peeling potatoes...

...and washing the sailors' smelly socks.

Finally, he'd had enough. He went to the captain and asked for a proper sailor's job.

Captain Winkle thought Sam was rather rude. But he decided to put him to the test.

"All right," he said, "Let's see you sail the ship into port!"

Sam's chest swelled with pride as he took the wheel.

But steering a ship wasn't as easy as it looked.

Luckily, the ship wasn't too badly damaged. Sam begged for one more chance.

"Very well," said Captain Winkle, at last. "You can guard the ship's treasure."

That night, while the rest of the sailors snored in their bunks, Sam sat guard.

But he was exhausted after his hard day's work. Soon, he was fast asleep as well.

Hours later, Sam was woken from his dreams by a wicked laugh.

He rushed up on deck, to see the dreaded Masked Pirate sailing off with Captain Winkle's treasure.

Sam felt terrible. What would the captain say? He didn't have to wait long to find out.

When Captain Winkle had calmed down, he offered a reward to whoever could track down the thief or his treasure.

But, as the pirate always wore a mask, no one knew what he looked like. Suddenly, Sam had an idea. "I'll find the pirate *and* your treasure," he said.

Captain Winkle didn't have much confidence in his cabin boy, but no one else had a plan.

That evening, Sam went to the Spyglass Inn, where the local pirates spent the night.

At breakfast next morning, Sam said in a loud voice, "I heard the Masked Pirate talking in his sleep last night. He described the exact spot where he hides his treasure!"

One particular pirate sitting in a corner began to look worried. Sam's plan was working.

"Now I know where the treasure is, I'm going to get it for myself!" Sam went on.

Hearing this, the pirate rushed out of the inn. Sam followed close behind.

The pirate jumped into a boat and rowed to an island just off the coast.

Sam ran to Captain Winkle, yelling, "Follow that pirate!"

When they arrived on the island, they found the pirate hurriedly digging up a treasure chest.

The captain recognized it at once. It was *his* treasure chest. Taking a flying leap, he landed on the pirate.

"Take my ship and fetch help, Sam my boy!" he roared.

"You trust me to sail?" cried Sam. He grinned from ear to ear. "Aye aye, Captain!" he said.

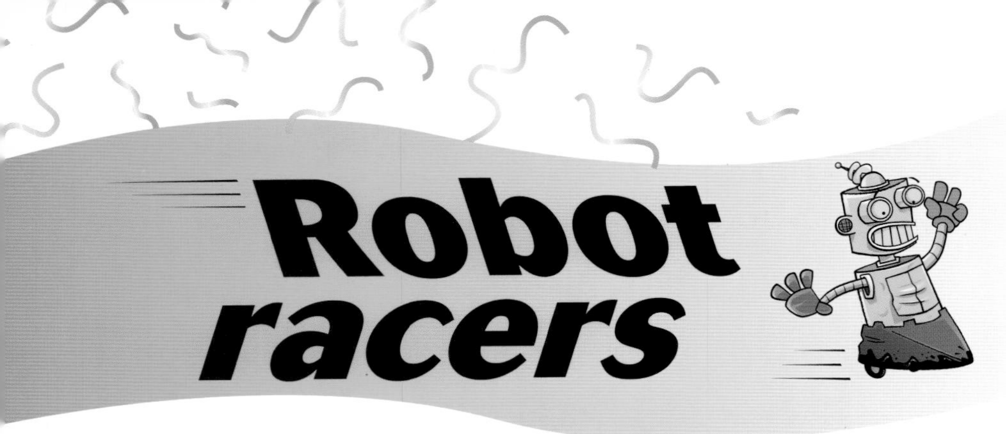

BOTSVILLE
ROAD RACE
TOMORROW
1st prize - a deluxe
robo-makeover

Squeaky the cleaning robot hated his job. He was out in all weather, sweeping streets. What he really wanted was to win the Botsville road race.

The winning robot would get a new memory chip and a head-to-wheel polish.

But Squeaky didn't dare enter. He was so rusty and clanky, he wasn't sure he could even finish the race.

He was feeling sorry for himself when a noisy robot zoomed past.

Out of the way,
rust bucket!

Tanktop was the biggest, meanest robot in town. Everyone was certain he would win tomorrow's big race.

Tanktop wasn't taking any chances. He had a plan to make sure none of the other racers even started.

That night, as the Botsville robots recharged themselves, Tanktop visited each of his rivals in secret.

HISSS!

He gave Tina Turbo a puncture...

stole Cyber Sid's memory chip...

undid Andi Droid's battery pack...

She'll sleep right through the race!

and reset Betty Byte's built-in alarm clock.

The next morning, Tanktop was the only robot at the starting line. It looked as if his plan had worked. The judge was puzzled. "Where is everyone?" he wondered.

"I'll take my prize now," smirked Tanktop.

"There must be someone else willing to race," cried the judge desperately. Tanktop was making him look stupid.

Just then a tinny voice piped up. "I will!"

Everyone in the crowd turned. "Is that Squeaky?" said someone in amazement.

What chance have you got?

"I'd like to try," said Squeaky. His joints were feeling especially stiff today, but he couldn't miss his chance.

"Very well," said the judge, with a sigh of relief. "Robots, on your marks!"

Tanktop hadn't bothered to charge up his battery that morning. But he was confident he could still beat Squeaky.

The robots set off on their lap of the town. Tanktop raced off with a roar and Squeaky clattered off in hot pursuit.

As soon as he was out of sight of the crowd, Tanktop opened a flap in his back.

"Ha ha!" he chuckled. "These nails will slow down that robo wreck!"

By the time Squeaky spotted the spiky trap, it was too late.

Luckily, Squeaky was so old that his wheels were made of solid rubber. They didn't burst and he was still in the race.

"I'll show that cheat!" thought Squeaky. He put on a burst of speed. Soon, he'd caught up with Tanktop.

"Let's see you get out of this!" boomed Tanktop, as he opened another compartment.

"Oil!" squealed Squeaky.

Squeaky shut his eyes and hoped for the best, as he slithered and slid all over the road.

CRASH!

Squeaky was left battered and dented, but at least he was still in one piece. He tried to get up and found he couldn't move. His joints were too stiff.

As he sat there, Squeaky realized what he needed was all around him. Unwinding his hose, he guzzled up every last drop of oil.

Soon, Squeaky was back on his rival's tail. Tanktop was running out of power fast.

But Tanktop still had one trick up his sleeve – his telescopic arms. He reached out to Squeaky's front wheel and undid the screw.

Sparks flew through the air as Squeaky's wheel bounced past Tanktop. In seconds, Squeaky had ground to a halt.

As the crowd came back into view, Tanktop used the last of his power to roar across the finishing line. "Ha ha, I've won!" he cried.

Tanktop was already boasting to the crowds as poor old Squeaky was carried across the line.

"Congratulations!" cried the judge as he shook Squeaky by the hand.

"Well, I suppose I almost won," Squeaky sniffed, sadly.

"Not almost," said the judge. "You **did** win. Look!"

He showed Squeaky and Tanktop the photograph taken at the finishing line.

"Your wheel crossed the line a second before Tanktop. That makes you the winner!"

Squeaky clunked with delight, the crowd cheered and Tanktop blew a fuse.

Sir Gawain and the Green Knight

It was New Year's Eve in the kingdom of Camelot and King Arthur was holding a feast. Everyone was eating, laughing and having fun when...

...a giant knight strode into the hall. He was as big as a bear and looked as wild as a wolf. But the strangest thing about him was – he was completely green.

The giant looked at King Arthur's knights, seated around the table. After a pause, he roared, "Which of you will play a New Year's game with me? You chop off my head, then I'll chop off yours!"

No one wanted to play his game. But the Green Knight refused to leave. Finally, Sir Gawain agreed. Seizing the giant's massive sword, he sliced off his green head.

Everyone gasped as the head bounced down the hall like a huge green ball.

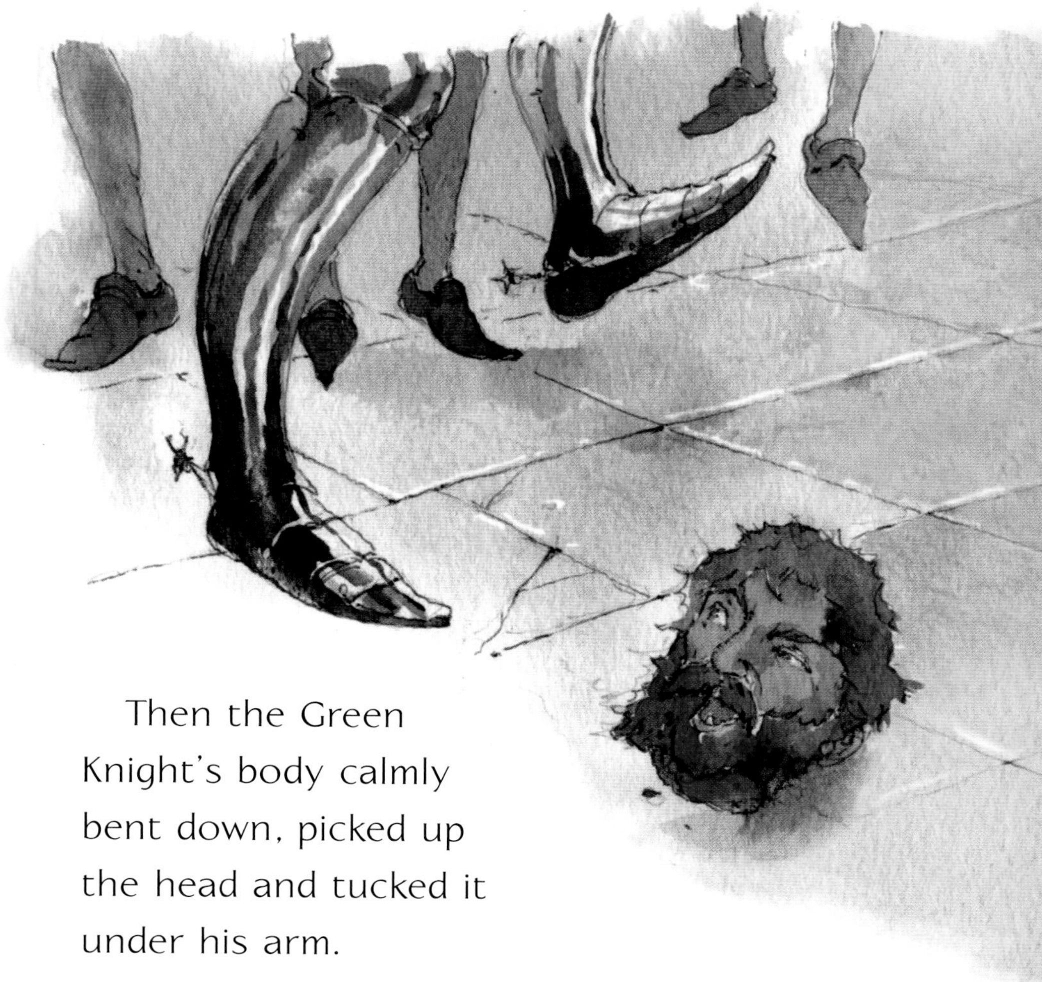

Then the Green Knight's body calmly bent down, picked up the head and tucked it under his arm.

The head looked up. "Well done, Sir Gawain!" it said. "Now it's my turn."

Sir Gawain turned pale.

"You have a year and a day," the head went on. "Meet me at the Green Chapel next New Year's Day."

But where's the
Green Chapel?
You must find
it yourself.

The following winter, Sir Gawain set off. He knew he was riding to certain death but he had given his word.

Can you tell me where to find the Green Chapel?
I've never heard of it.

He searched the kingdom with no success. By Christmas he was exhausted, but he would not give up.

At last, Sir Gawain came to a castle in a forest, owned by the lord Sir Bertilak. Sir Gawain asked his question and Sir Bertilak smiled.

"The Green Chapel?" he said. "It's just around the corner."

"Finally!" sighed Gawain.

When Sir Bertilak heard Sir Gawain's story, he asked the knight to stay with him. For three days, Sir Bertilak went out hunting. Gawain stayed at home with Bertilak's wife.

In the evenings, they ate dinner together. The knights told each other everything they had done during the day.

"I chased a stag!" said Bertilak, on the first night.

Gawain blushed. "I read to your wife and she gave me a kiss," he said.

"I chased a boar!" said Bertilak on the second night.

"Your wife kissed me twice," said Gawain, bright red.

"I chased a fox!" said Bertilak on the third night.

"Your wife gave me three kisses," Gawain whispered.

But Gawain kept a secret. Sir Bertilak's wife had also given him a magic belt. She said it could save his life.

Gawain knew he should tell Bertilak. But he wanted to wear it when he met the Green Knight.

On New Year's Day, Sir Gawain rode to the Green Chapel. The Green Knight was waiting. Telling Gawain to kneel down, he raised his massive sword...

But then he lowered his sword again.

The Green Knight raised his sword for a second time. Again, he put it down.

The third time he raised his sword, Sir Gawain didn't worry. But this time, the Green Knight gave Gawain a painful nick on the neck.

"Why did you do that?" asked Gawain.

The next minute, the giant started to shrink...

and shrink...

until he turned into...

Sir Bertilak!

"Yes!" cried Sir Bertilak. "I was the Green Knight. It was a test. I know you're brave because you came to seek me. But I wanted to see how honest a knight you were, too."

"So, I asked my wife to kiss you and give you the belt," Sir Bertilak went on. "Twice, you told me the truth and I didn't harm you. But the third time you kept a secret."

Sir Gawain fell to his knees. "I'm a bad knight," he said. "I'm a coward. You should cut off my head."

"Nonsense!" said Sir Bertilak. "You didn't do that badly. Now, come back to the castle. I've organized a feast."

Gawain smiled, feeling incredibly relieved.

"Oh, and no more games, I promise!" Sir Bertilak chuckled.

The bed monster's secret

Ben Boggle lay awake in a cold sweat. How could he sleep with a monster under his bed?

Every evening it was the same story. As soon as Ben switched off his bedside light, the monster woke with a snort.

Grrrgggh
Grugglugggle

All through the night, the creature gurgled and growled in the shadows.

Ben had never dared to look under his bed. He was too terrified of what he might see.

Perhaps the monster had ten eyes...

or long, slimy tentacles...

or huge, sharp teeth...

or all of these!

At school, Ben could hardly keep his eyes open.

"Wake up, Ben Boggle!" yelled his teacher.

"That's the third time this week you've fallen asleep in class." Mr. Grizzle liked people to be awake in his mathematics lessons.

Even when he was wide awake, Ben was hopeless with numbers. When he felt sleepy, they were even more difficult.

"Get to bed earlier, young man," said Mr. Grizzle, in a stern voice.

Unless Ben could get rid of the monster, Mr. Grizzle would be shouting at him every day.

Tired and worried, Ben was walking home when he spotted something in a shop window.

"Maybe that book has something about bed monsters," Ben thought. He dashed inside.

As soon as he got home, Ben read the book from cover to cover. But there was no mention of monsters under the bed.

Chapter XII
What monsters eat
Monsters like to eat:
• little kids
• monster hunters
• small furry animals
• big furry animals
• chocolate chip cookies

"What a waste of money," thought Ben. Then he had an idea. Perhaps the book could help him after all...

Ben decided to build a monster trap. He raided the chocolate chip cookie jar and took a net from his dad's fishing box. In no time at all, his trap was ready.

That night, he climbed into bed, switched off the light and waited.

At first, Ben's room was spookily silent. Then he heard a crunching, munching sound followed by a whoosh. His monster trap had worked!

Nervously, Ben crept over to the net. But nothing could have prepared him for what happened next...

"Please don't hurt me," squeaked a tiny voice. The smallest monster in the world was tangled in the net.

"I can't believe I was scared of you," cried Ben.

"I know," the monster said sadly. "I'm too small to scare anyone. That's why I hid under your bed. I didn't want you to see me."

"I'm the most useless monster alive," she wailed and started to sob. Ben began to feel sorry for the strange little creature.

The monster sniffed. "It's impossible to scare people when you only weigh fifteen ounces," she said. "I mean, that's less than half a kilo."

"Is it really?" said Ben.

"Oh yes," replied the monster. "I may be small, but I'm not stupid."

This gave Ben such a great idea that he grinned all night, even in his sleep.

He was still grinning the next day at school as Mr. Grizzle began the lesson.

"Ben Boggle," barked Mr. Grizzle. "What is nine times eight?"

"Seventy two," said Ben, confidently.

Mr. Grizzle couldn't believe his ears. "Oh, that's correct," he said, shakily. He asked Ben problem after problem. Ben answered every one correctly.

Mr. Grizzle was amazed.

"Well done, Ben," he said. "What an astonishing improvement!"

Luckily, no one but Ben had heard the tiny voice whispering the answers.

Ben smiled to himself. Mathematics is a lot easier when you have a monster in your pocket.

Jon and the green troll

Once, there was a poor farmer. His wife was dead. He lived with his only son, Jon, near the mountains in Scotland.

In the spring and summer, Jon and his father worked hard in the fields.

This tree just
won't budge!

In the autumn, they shut up the farm and went down to the sea, to fish.

But, one year, Jon's father felt too old for the trip. "You'll have to go alone," he said to Jon.

Take good care of yourself!
Don't worry, I will!

"Just remember one thing," his father warned. "Don't stop at the big, black rock. That's where the trolls live."

As Jon drove up a rocky mountain path, the sky grew dark. Then a storm blew up. Lightning flashed and thunder growled. "I wish my dad were here," thought Jon.

At last, he saw a big, black rock. "Ah! I can shelter there," he thought.

Jon had forgotten his father's warning. He was just glad to be out of the storm. He sat down outside a cave and unpacked his sack.

Whew!
That journey made
me really hungry!

"Time for supper," he said to himself. He had crusty bread, smelly cheese, an apple and a very big fish. "Delicious!" he said, as he chomped away.

Suddenly, Jon heard a noise coming from inside the cave. He was so scared, he stopped chewing.

He could hear voices – babies' voices! "Wahhh!" they cried. "We're hungry!"

Jon quickly picked up the fish and cut it in half. He threw both halves into the cave. "Here, eat these!" he called.

The crying stopped at once.

"Whew," said Jon. "Thank goodness for that."

He was almost asleep when a giant shadow fell over him. Jon looked up. A troll! A troll was coming for him.

"I smell a man!" said a low, rumbling voice.

Now, Jon remembered his father's warning. But it was too late.

The troll came over to Jon and picked him up. He shook with terror. This was his first fishing trip alone – and he was the one to be caught. "Please, don't eat me!" he begged.

But the troll was gentle. "Don't be scared," she said. "I want to thank you for feeding my children."

The troll took Jon into her cave and looked after him. She even gave him her children's bed. It was lumpy but Jon slept well.

The next morning, after breakfast, the troll waved Jon off.

"Take these magic fishing hooks," she said. "When you reach the sea, look for an old man named Charlie. You must go fishing with him."

"Thank you," said Jon. "I will."

"But only fish near the pointed rock," the troll warned.

Jon did just as the troll had said. He found Charlie in an old hut by the beach.

"Will you come fishing with me?" asked Jon.

"Are you sure?" asked Charlie. "I'm the worst fisherman in the world. I never catch anything!"

Charlie showed Jon his boat. It was full of holes and falling to pieces.

"Don't worry!" said Jon. "I can soon fix that."

He set to work with some tar and planks of wood. Soon, the boat was as good as new.

"Let's row to that pointed rock," Jon said to Charlie. They put worms on the magic hooks, and started to fish. "Hey!" Jon cried, a few seconds later. "I've caught one!"

"So have I!" shouted Charlie.

And another!

They couldn't believe their luck. The boat was full of fish!

The other fishermen couldn't believe it either. "What's your secret?" they asked.

Jon told them to fish near the pointed rock. But, when they tried, they didn't catch a thing.

Every day for the entire winter, Jon's magic hooks caught hundreds of fish. "They've done it again!" gasped a local fisherman.

"Charlie's lucky at last!" said another, shaking his head in disbelief.

Every day, Jon and Charlie cleaned the fish and hung them up to dry. They had more fish than all the other fishermen put together.

"There's something fishy going on here," one of them grumbled.

When spring came, it was time for Jon to go home. On the way, he visited the troll and gave her half his fish. "I never could have caught them without you," he said.

"Thank you," she said. "One day, you'll have a dream about me. When you do, you must come back to my cave."

Back at home, Jon helped his father on the farm. A year later, he had a dream about the troll – just as she had said. "I have to go and visit someone," he told his dad.

He quickly left for her cave, without telling his father where he was going.

At last, he reached the cave. He peered inside.

"Hello?" he called. "Is anybody home?"

There was no answer.

Jon crept into the cave. It was empty except for two chests.

"Are they for me?" Jon wondered. What could be inside?

He put the chests on his cart and took them home. When he opened them, he found piles of treasure and gold. Jon and his father were so rich, they never had to work again. "Hip hip hooray!" they cheered.

Jon never told his father where the money came from.

The tale of the haunted TV

One Saturday afternoon, Glen Goggle was watching TV. Suddenly the set made a funny fizzing noise and the screen went black.

Glen's dad called out Mr. Sparks, the TV repairman.

"You've worn it out, lad," said Mr. Sparks.

"It wasn't my fault!" said Glen.

Mr. Sparks put the television in his van and returned with a battered-looking replacement.

Glen had never seen such an ancient TV set.

"It's better than nothing," said Mr. Goggle.

Glen's parents had no problems watching the TV. But the first time that Glen tuned in, something odd happened. A man in strange clothes appeared on the screen and burst into song.

"This isn't Cartoon Club," muttered Glen.

"Welcome, one and all, to the world of Harry Hall!" sang the man on the TV. Harry was a terrible singer. But he was so funny, Glen didn't mind missing the cartoons.

The next time Glen switched on, Harry appeared again. This time he was dressed as a magician.

This show was even funnier than the last. Every trick Harry did went wrong.

Oh dear!

Oops!

Oh no.

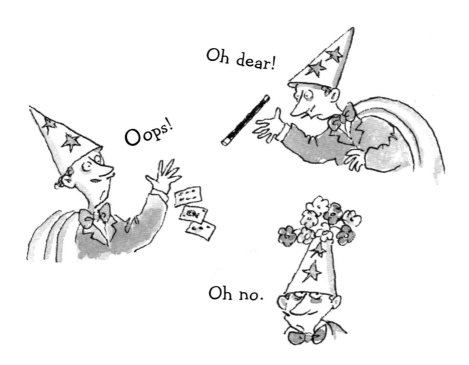

The useless magician made Glen laugh so much, he had to turn off the TV to stop his sides from aching.

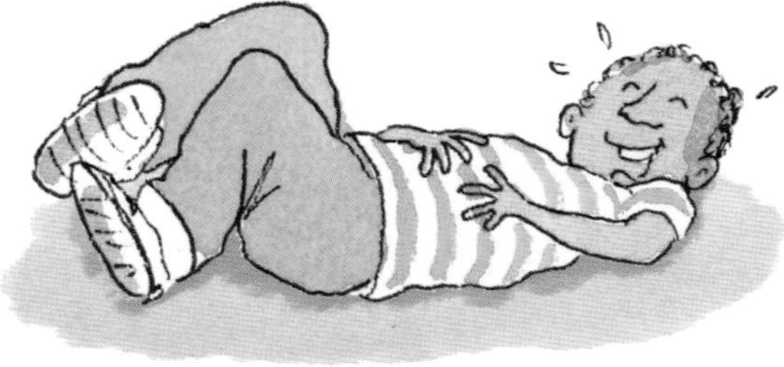

Next day, Harry tried to dance and kept tripping over his own feet. Although Harry was funny, Glen was starting to miss the cartoons.

Glen was about to switch channels, when Harry fell forward – right through the TV screen. Then he grew to full size before Glen's astonished eyes.

"Sorry," panted Harry. "I should have taken more dance lessons when I was alive."

Glen gulped. "You mean, you're a g...g..."

"I always wanted to be on television," said Harry. "So when I became a ghost, I decided to haunt this set."

"You were very funny," said Glen.

"I didn't mean to be," Harry replied.

"I can't rest easy in the spirit world until I'm a star," he sighed.

Glen felt sorry for Harry. He offered to let him stay if he stopped haunting the TV.

Harry spent the next few days moping in Glen's room.

Then one afternoon, Glen showed him a ticket. "Look where we're going," he said, with a grin.

Come and watch
TALENT TIME
The Top TV Talent Contest
being recorded
Saturday October 4 at 3:00pm
at XYZ TV Studios
BIG CASH PRIZE FOR THE TOP ACT!

Harry was full of excitement. He'd never seen a TV show being made before.

Glen wasn't sure if spooks were allowed in TV studios. Harry shrank himself down so Glen could smuggle him inside.

Glen was relieved when he reached his seat in the audience. Harry peeked out as the lights dimmed and the show began.

There were singers, dancers and comedians. Glen thought they were great, but Harry did nothing but grumble. "I could do better than that!" he complained.

"Shh!" said Glen, who was getting some funny looks from the woman beside them.

Glen didn't notice the ghost float away. So he got a shock when a full-size Harry suddenly appeared on stage.

Harry pushed the other contestants aside and went into his act.

He sang terrible songs...

he messed up his magic tricks...

and he finished with his clumsy dance routine.

The audience roared with laughter. Harry won first prize as the star of the show. He called Glen on stage to say thank you.

With a big grin on his face, Harry faded away.

Glen grinned too. Harry had given him the prize money to buy a brand new TV.

The band of robbers

Pinchbeck the wizard and Pogo the goblin were walking together in the woods.

They were talking about a magic spell.

"The mushrooms must be picked at midnight," Pogo told Pinchbeck.

They were so busy talking, they didn't see a robber creeping up behind them.

Suddenly, the robber jumped out. He hit Pinchbeck over the head with his club.

"Give me your gold!" he shouted.

Pinchbeck dropped the gold. Pogo just ran.

The robber tied Pinchbeck to a tree. Three hours later, Pogo came back.

"My head hurts," groaned Pinchbeck.

"Let's go to the castle for help," said Pogo.

Slowly, Pinchbeck and Pogo climbed to the castle. They stopped in front of a huge wooden door and knocked.

Inside, the king and queen were having tea.

"Was that a knock?" asked the queen, pausing between mouthfuls of soft-boiled egg.

"Hmm, I wonder who it could be?" said the king.

"Who's there?" called the king.

"Pogo!" said Pogo. "With Pinchbeck the wizard."

"We were robbed in the woods. Please let us in."

"That's terrible!" said the king. "Come in at once."

The queen made some fresh tea, and wrapped Pinchbeck's head in bandages.

"The robbers came here too," she said.

"And they're coming back tomorrow," the king added. "If we don't give them two more bags of gold, they'll take over our castle. And we don't have any gold left!"

That night, Pinchbeck and Pogo stayed in the castle. They wished that they could do something to help.

"My head's thumping too much," sighed Pinchbeck. "I can't think of any spells."

But Pogo had an idea. Early the next morning, he sneaked out of the castle. "I hope I don't wake anyone up," he thought.

He found two sacks in a shed and tiptoed through the garden.

If he tried hard enough, he might be able to work a spell. As fast as he could, he stuffed both sacks with leaves.

Then he hurried back to the castle.

When Pinchbeck saw the sacks, he clapped his hands with glee. “Pogo! You’ve helped me to remember a spell!”

Umpi-grumpi, do as as you’re told.
Fool those robbers and turn into gold!

Yellow smoke filled the air, then...

Rat-a-tat-tat! The robbers were banging on the door.

"Open up!" they yelled. "We know you don't have any gold. The castle's ours!"

The queen began to cry. "But we have nowhere to go," she sobbed.

"Tough!" said the robbers.

"Please don't take the castle," pleaded the king.

Just then, the robbers heard another voice. It was Pinchbeck. "Take a look at this," he called, waving at the robbers.

They couldn't believe their eyes. The robbers blinked, and stared, then blinked again.

"Take your gold," said Pinchbeck. "And make sure we never see you here again."

"Ha! We're rich now," said the chief robber. "Why would we come back?"

And they set off. They rode for five days and five nights. The sacks were getting lighter but the robbers didn't notice. At last, they stopped to rest.

Tired and hungry, they decided to cheer themselves up. "Let's count our gold," they said.

But all they found in the sacks were....

"It's a trick!" shouted the chief robber, "We'll go back!"

But it was no good. They'd come too far and were completely lost.

At the castle, Pinchbeck's head healed and his spells returned. It was time to go.

But before he left, he gave the king and queen a magic sack of gold which would never run out.

Then he and Pogo headed back into the woods, the way they had come.

Sinbad the sailor

Long ago, in the city of Baghdad, Sinbad lived with his father, a rich merchant. When the merchant died, he left Sinbad his whole fortune.

Sinbad was so rich, he didn't need to work. Instead, he spent his money on fine clothes and wild parties.

One day, he was shocked to find his purse empty. "I can't believe I've spent my fortune!" he said to himself.

He decided to follow in his father's footsteps and sell things for a living. First, he sold his house. Then he bought some expensive silks and spices and went down to the port.

A group of merchants were busy loading their ship. They invited Sinbad to join them and he jumped on board.

After a week at sea, they dropped anchor by a sandy island. They were cooking supper over a fire, when the ground began to tremble.

"The island's moving!" a sailor cried.

"It's not an island!" yelled another.

"We're on a whale!" cried the captain and swam to the ship.

The others were flung into the sea as the whale flipped its tail and dived underwater.

Many men drowned, but Sinbad was lucky. He clung on to a wooden chest and floated through the night. At dawn, he landed on the shore of a distant island.

A man on horseback spotted Sinbad and took him to see his ruler, King Mahrajan.

Sinbad told the king about the whale. "Now I'm stranded far from home," he sighed.

"Work for me and I'll look after you," said the king.

One day, Sinbad was on duty at the port, when a captain came up to him.

"Sir, where can I sell these silks and spices?" he asked.

Sinbad was amazed. "I had some silk like that..." he said.

"Well, these silks belonged to a merchant called Sinbad," said the captain.

"I *am* Sinbad," cried Sinbad.

The captain was amazed, but he gave Sinbad his silks and spices. After selling them at an excellent price, Sinbad joined the captain's ship and set sail for Baghdad.

At first, Sinbad was delighted to be home. But soon he had itchy feet. He wanted to visit new places. So he bought more silks and spices to trade.

A friendly captain welcomed him on board his ship and they headed for the high seas.

One day, they stopped at a deserted island to collect fresh water. Sinbad sat down in a shady spot and fell asleep.

An hour later, he woke in a panic. The ship had set sail without him. He was stranded.

Sinbad climbed a tree and looked over the island. All he could see was one huge, white egg. As Sinbad watched, a gigantic roc bird flew onto the egg and settled down to sleep.

Sinbad knew the roc bird was very strong. Maybe it could rescue him. He unwound his turban, crept up to the bird and tied himself to its leg.

When the roc woke up, it stretched its giant wings and soared into the sky.

Sinbad found himself dangling high above the clouds.

Before long, the roc dived down into a deep valley. Sinbad felt hard ground beneath his feet and quickly untied himself.

The roc caught a sheep in its claws and flew away. Sinbad stared in fear at the steep-sided valley. It was squirming with snakes, which slithered over dead sheep.

Then Sinbad noticed the ground was studded with jewels. He was stuffing some in his pockets, when he saw a vicious snake eyeing him hungrily.

Sinbad ducked down. How could he escape? Seeing the rocs circling overhead gave him an idea...

Quickly, he tied himself to a sheep and waited. In no time, a roc swooped down and grabbed the sheep in its claws. It flew out of the valley, with Sinbad trailing below.

The roc landed on a cliff. It was about to eat the sheep, when a group of men charged at the bird, scaring it away.

"Bother!" said one. "No jewels in *this* sheep's wool."

Then they spotted Sinbad. His escape from snake valley amazed them. In return for some jewels, they put him on a ship bound for Baghdad.

Once more, Sinbad was delighted to be home. But the feeling didn't last long. This time, he traded a bag of jewels for silks and spices to sell.

His third journey went well and land was in sight when a bunch of short, ugly and very hairy men ambushed the ship. One by one, the hairy men threw the merchants overboard, then sailed away.

The miserable merchants were washed onto a beach.

They explored the new shore and found a courtyard filled with pots and firewood.

But the courtyard was owned by a greedy giant, who licked his lips when he saw his visitors. Before they could blink, he roasted a fat merchant.

After supper, the giant fell asleep – across the only exit.

"Don't worry," whispered Sinbad. "When he leaves, we'll take his firewood and make a raft so we can escape."

At dawn, the giant woke up, heaved himself to his feet and left. The men hurried to the beach, where they tied the firewood together with vines.

As they pushed off from the shore, they heard a big splash. The angry giant was pelting the raft with rocks. Seconds later, a rock smashed the raft to pieces.

Most of the men drowned, but Sinbad and two others were lucky. They survived by clinging onto a log. But by noon, they had fainted under the hot sun.

The next thing they knew, they had drifted onto a stony beach and a huge snake had wound itself around them. It eyed the three men, opened its mouth wide and swallowed Sinbad's two friends.

Sinbad didn't dare move until the snake had slithered off.

He gazed out to sea, praying for a ship to arrive... and one did! Better still, Sinbad recognized the captain from his second journey.

"You left me behind!" said Sinbad, angrily.

"I'm sorry," said the man. "Let me make it up to you. I'll take you home right away!"

Within a week, Sinbad was back in Baghdad.

"Home again!" cried Sinbad. But it didn't take long before he was back at the market, buying silks and spices.

He joined another merchant ship and traded his goods from port to port.

One day, a sudden gale whipped up the waves. Water came crashing onto the deck and smashed up the ship.

Sinbad and seven other merchants were luckier than the rest. They clung onto the broken mast and drifted to a far-off shore.

Some islanders found the men and took them to their king.

"Welcome," said the king. "Please join us for a feast."

They were all starving, except for Sinbad. He just watched as the others gobbled down food like pigs. To his horror, the hungry men actually turned into slurping, guzzling animals.

"Stop eating!" Sinbad cried, but the men no longer understood him. An islander rounded up Sinbad's friends and herded them through the door.

Sinbad hid in a dark corner. When no one was looking, he fled from the palace grounds.

He ran straight past the herd of men, who were grazing in a field. And he didn't stop until he'd reached the other side of the island.

There, he couldn't believe his luck. A ship was sailing close to shore. He waved at it wildly and the captain waved back. Soon, Sinbad was heading for Baghdad again.

The problem was Sinbad found life at home dull after his adventures. One morning he saw a beautiful new ship at the port and decided to buy it.

He loaded the ship with silks and spices, hired an eager crew and set sail.

They came to an island with another roc's egg. Some sailors were curious and went to see it. They threw stones at the egg to see how tough it was. Fifty stones later, it cracked.

"Fools!" cried Sinbad. "The mother roc will want revenge!"

As they sailed away, a dark shape hid the sun. It was a roc! She dropped a massive boulder on the ship and all but Sinbad perished in the sea.

Yet again, Sinbad was saved. This time, he was swept to a leafy island. As he paused for water by a stream, he saw a sad troll.

Sinbad helped the troll cross the stream. But then the troll refused to get down from Sinbad's shoulders. It just tightened its grip around his neck.

For days, Sinbad was the troll's prisoner. He carried it everywhere until he was exhausted. Then he remembered he had a flask of wine.

The troll saw Sinbad take a sip and snatched the flask. It glugged down the wine and was soon swaying from side to side. A few burps later, it toppled to the ground.

Sinbad ran away and met some people carrying baskets. "Can you help me get to Baghdad?" he asked hurriedly.

"If you help us collect more coconuts," replied a bald man.

"How?" wondered Sinbad, following the group into a forest of palms. Monkeys chattered in every tree.

"Watch!" said the man. He picked up a stone and threw it at a monkey. The monkey was very annoyed and threw a coconut back at the man.

"Hey, that nearly hit me!" muttered Sinbad.

Soon, all the monkeys were throwing coconuts. Sinbad easily collected enough to pay for his trip home.

For a while, Sinbad was happy simply lazing around at home. Then some merchants came to visit and their tales of travel filled Sinbad with envy.

He set sail once more, trading from port to port...

...until one night, the ship sailed off course. In the gloom, no one saw sharp rocks ahead. The ship was smashed to pieces and only Sinbad and four others reached the shore.

They searched the craggy island from top to bottom and found nothing but rocks and water. One by one, the men starved to death.

Before long, Sinbad was the only man left. He sat by a river, feeling very alone.

Then he noticed something strange. The river was flowing into a cave, not out to sea.

Sinbad had an idea. "I'll make a raft," he thought, "and hope the river leads me to some food."

The riverbed sparkled with jewels, so he took a few handfuls before floating off.

His raft glided into the cave and sped up, hurtling through darkness. All Sinbad could hear was the whoosh of water. Had his luck finally run out?

The next thing he knew, he was lying on a sunny bank. He looked up to see a crowd gathered around him.

A local merchant gave Sinbad some food and, in return for several jewels, sent him on a ship to Baghdad.

Back home, Sinbad's jewels bought him all kinds of treats. But, guess what? Sinbad still wasn't content.

"Soon I'll be too old to travel," he thought.

So he set out on a final journey. He was aboard a merchant ship in the China Sea when a terrible storm blew up.

A monster whale surged up through the waves. As it got closer, it opened its massive jaws and swallowed the ship in one gulp.

Luckily, Sinbad managed to jump overboard just in time. The storm died down and, once again, he drifted to a strange shore. "Safe again. I don't know how I do it," he thought.

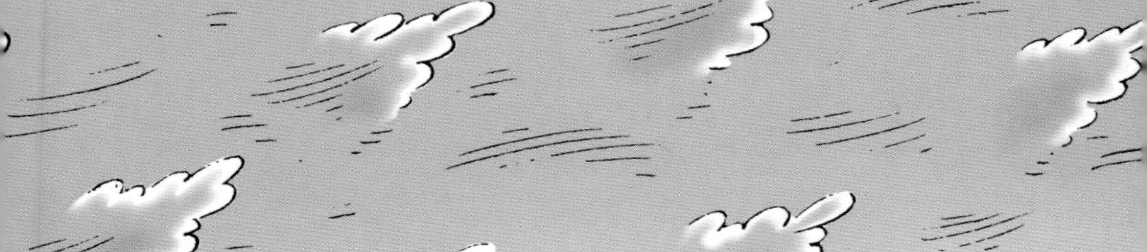

As he wandered through an exotic forest, he found a river flowing into a cave.

"Aha! I'll build another raft," thought Sinbad.

But this river carried him through darkness to a steep waterfall.

"I'm a dead man!" Sinbad screamed, as he started falling.

Suddenly, he stopped – in mid-air.

A surprised old man had caught him in a net.

"You need to dry off!" said the man, and he took Sinbad home with him.

The old man asked his daughter, Emira, to fetch some clothes. Sinbad gazed at her open-mouthed. He had never seen such a lovely woman.

Emira's father thought Sinbad was charming and invited him to stay. Over the next few weeks, Emira and Sinbad fell in love.

With the old man's blessing, the couple married.

A year later, Emira's father died of old age, leaving her and Sinbad a fortune.

"Why don't we go sailing?" said Sinbad. "We could buy some silks and spices to trade."

"Ooh, yes!" replied Emira, who had always wanted to travel.

After months at sea, they found themselves in Baghdad.

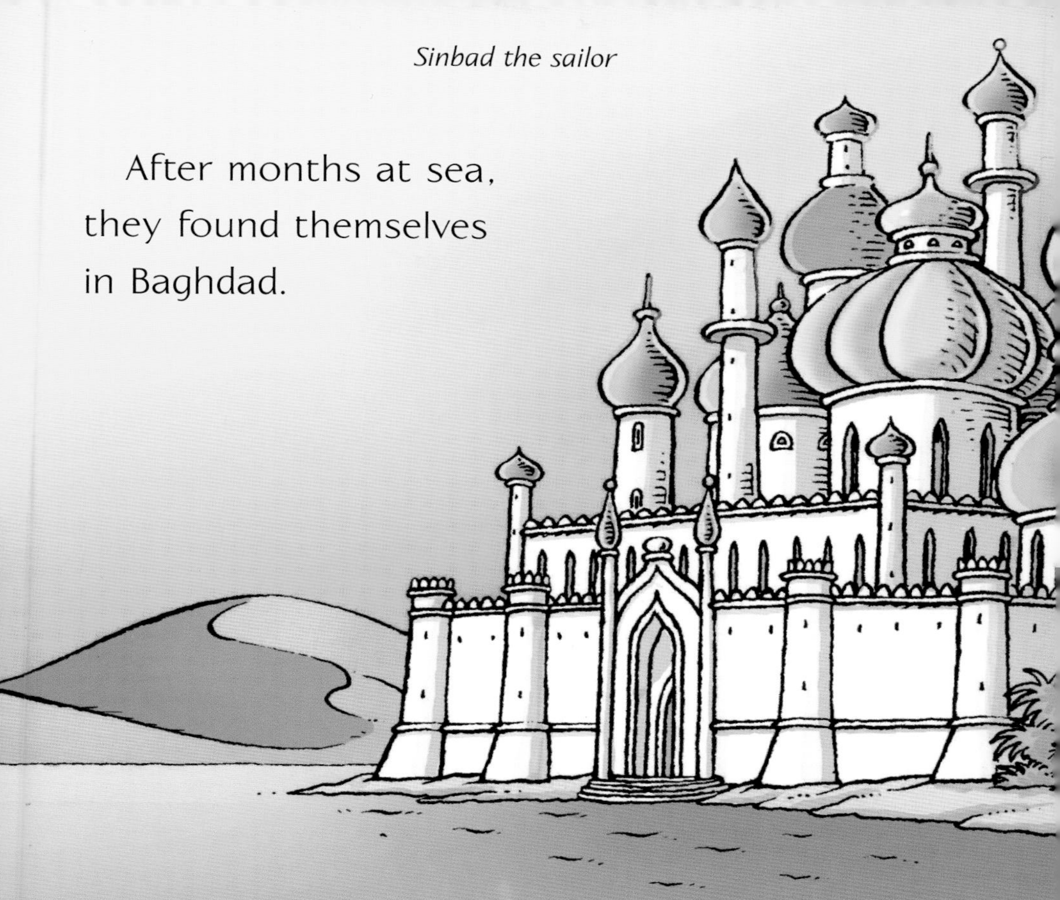

"What a gorgeous city!" cried Emira.

"Isn't it!" agreed Sinbad. He was delighted to be home... at least for a while.

Victor saves the village

Victor made barrels, the best barrels in the country.

He made the best barrels because he used the best wood. He hunted hard to find the tallest, straightest trees.

He was always looking out for the perfect tree. So he didn't always watch where he was going. One day, he tripped and fell...

...into a cave.

Try as he might...

Almost there!

Aaaaargh!

...Victor couldn't climb out of the cave.

Suddenly, he heard a deep growl. There was something behind him! Victor looked. He wished he hadn't.

"Please don't eat me!" Victor begged.

"We won't," said one of the dragons. "Not yet. We're going to sleep. Wake us up in the spring."

Victor was stuck. Soon, he was bored as well.

There was nothing he could do.

He had to wait until spring.

All he had to eat and drink were grass and water. After a while, he was no longer as round as a barrel. He was as thin as a twig.

Finally, the dragons awoke.

"We can't eat you!" said one. "You're skin and bone."

"Grab my tail," the other dragon said to Victor. "We'll take you home. Perhaps your friends will make a juicy meal."

The villagers were amazed to see Victor after so long, and they were terrified to see the dragons.

But before the dragons could bite anyone, Victor invited them to a huge feast.

Victor and the dragons ate for a week. The dragons enjoyed the food so much, they decided they would never eat people again.

The villagers were very pleased to hear it. They put up a statue of Victor in the market square.

Now, everyone who visits knows how Victor saved the village from two hungry dragons.

Now he always looks where he's going!

The terrible Tidybot

"Luke, you're the laziest boy in the world!" cried Mrs. Lively. His room was so untidy, she could hardly get in.

"Look at all this mess!" sighed Luke's mother as she clambered over a pile of books, clothes and toys.

"All you do all day is play on that beeping computer," said Mrs. Lively, crossly.

Luke wasn't listening. He had just reached level twelve on ***Android Attack***. Now he needed to concentrate.

"I've had just about enough, young man!" snapped Mrs. Lively.

"You have one week to clean up this room or the computer goes," she threatened. "I mean it!"

Luke heard ***that*** loud and clear. He couldn't possibly live without his computer. But cleaning his room would take forever. "I need someone to help me clean up," he thought.

He spent the next two hours searching the Internet for cleaning companies. They were all too expensive.

Luke had almost given up hope, when an advertisement popped up on the screen.

"That's just what I need," cried Luke. "It can clean my room, then I'll send it back."

Just under a week later, the Tidybot arrived at Luke's house. He managed to sneak the box up to his room, before his mother dashed past on her way out.

"I want that room clean by the time I come back!" she shouted. The front door slammed behind her. Luke had just two hours.

He ran to his room and excitedly tore open the box.

First, he read the instruction booklet. Then he aimed the remote control. The Tidybot was ready for action.

Luke pressed a red button twice and the robot jerked to life.

In minutes, all Luke's underpants, shirts and socks were off the floor and neatly put away. Luke was impressed.

He pressed button after button. The robot whizzed around the room, obeying every command.

In no time at all, the bedroom was cleaner than it had ever been. Luke couldn't wait to see his mother's face when she returned.

He took a step back to admire the Tidybot's work. As he did, he heard a loud crack.

The remote control was bent and broken. "How can I return it now?" he thought.

But Luke had more important things to worry about. Breaking the control unit had made the Tidybot go crazy.

ALLOW ME TO PUT YOUR BOOKS ON THE SHELF SIR.

It hurtled around the room until it was messier than ever.

Before Luke could stop it, the rampaging robot zoomed out of his bedroom and down the stairs.

It went through every room in the house, leaving a messy trail behind.

Finally, the robot's battery went flat and it ground to a halt. Luke stared at the house in horror. What would his mother say?

He spent the next hour sweeping, mopping and polishing. Then he repacked the robot and hid it in the shed.

When he'd finished, he was so tired that he went to his bedroom to lie down. He was in for a shock. "Oh no, I completely forgot about my room!" he said.

As he slumped onto his bed in despair, his mother returned.

"Look at this room!" she cried. But Luke was so exhausted, he didn't hear.

Mrs. Lively shook her head as she carried off Luke's computer. "You really *are* the laziest boy in the world!" she said.

The story of Shiverham Hall
Shiverham Hall
Have a frightful stay, madam!

Shiverham Hall was a hotel with a difference. All the guests were dead.

Ghosts came from the spirit world to be greeted by Shiverham's spooky staff.

There were twenty-two ice-cold bedrooms...

a poltergeist-powered jacuzzi...

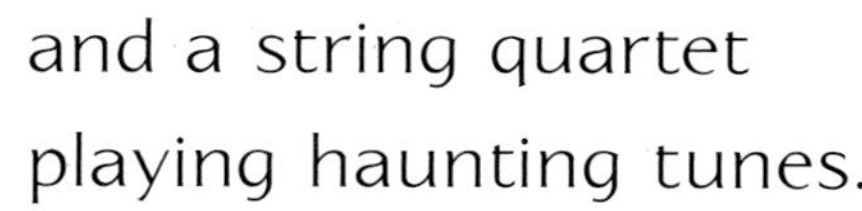

and a string quartet playing haunting tunes.

No living soul dared visit the hotel. It was far too creepy. The ghosts were left in peace.

Then, one afternoon, the hotel's deathly hush was shattered.

Most of the ghosts were napping. Mr. Quiver, the hotel manager, had come down for a glass of water.

Suddenly, a round-faced man flung open the front door and strode up to the reception desk.

"This is just what I've been looking for," he boomed.

A tall, thin man scuttled in after him.

"Um, are you sure, Mr. Slate?" he asked nervously.

"Of course I'm sure, Simkins," barked Slate. "This will make the perfect site for my new hotel. I've had it all designed."

Slate proudly spread out a large plan in front of his assistant. Behind them, Mr. Quiver sneaked up to get a better look.

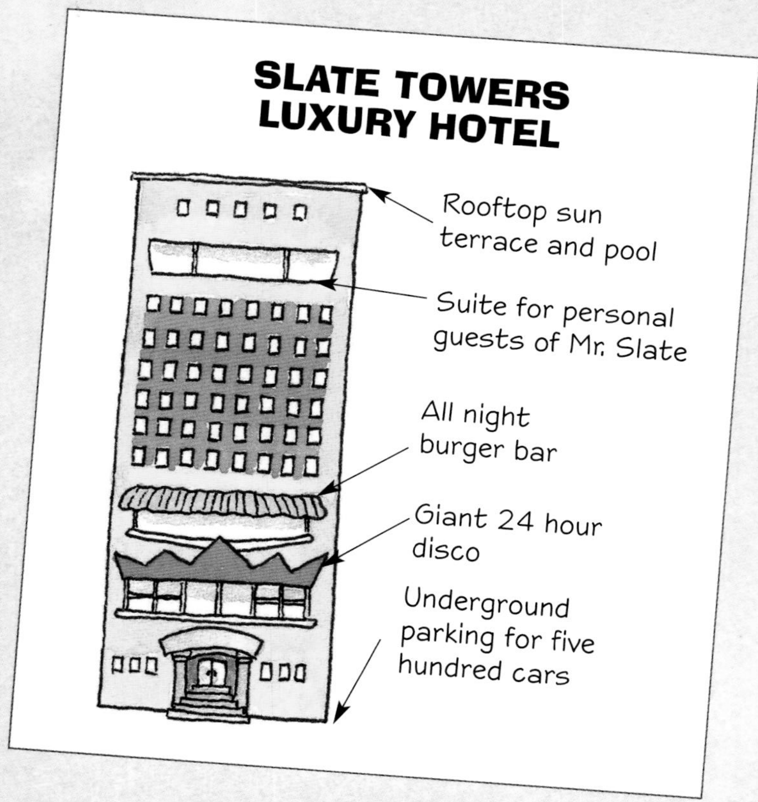

SLATE TOWERS
LUXURY HOTEL
Rooftop sun terrace and pool
Suite for personal guests of Mr. Slate
All night burger bar
Giant 24 hour disco
Underground parking for five hundred cars

Mr. Quiver was horrified.

"I'll have this place demolished in no time," Slate went on. "But perhaps I'll look around and see if there's anything worth saving first."

"Don't be too long," gulped Simkins. "They say the place is haunted."

"Ridiculous!" cried Slate. "Ghosts don't exist. And I'll stay the night to prove it."

"We don't exist, eh?" thought Mr. Quiver, as he floated upstairs.

Minutes later, he gathered the hotel staff together. No one was happy about Slate's plans.

"We'll never get any peace in his noisy new hotel," wailed Charlie the waiter.

"And where will our ghostly guests go?" asked Elsie the maid.

"Slate will have to be frightened off," said Mr. Quiver. "As soon as it gets dark, we'll start haunting."

Slate was climbing the rickety stairs to bed, when Mr. Quiver appeared in front of him.

Slate looked a little surprised. But then he shrugged. "Out of my way, potato head!" he shouted.

Mr. Quiver had never been so insulted in his life. Or his death.

But the ghosts weren't finished yet. As Slate brushed his teeth, Igor the porter popped up through the plughole.

The staff didn't give up. That night, Slate was visited by a stream of ghosts...

Elsie brought the bed sheets to life.

Charlie rattled a ghostly tea tray next to Slate's pillow.

Cora the cook sent possessed pots flying through the air.

Even the hotel guests tried to put the shivers up the unwelcome visitor.

Sir Gauntlet showed off his battle scars.

Lord Doublet lost his head.

And Miss Gauntly, the wailing lady, moaned the entire night.

But none of them could raise a single goosebump.

Next morning, Mr. Quiver listened in on Slate's meeting with Simkins.

"You were right," said Slate. "This place *is* full of ghosts."

"R..r..really?" stuttered Simkins, nervously. "So you'll forget your plans?"

“No way!” said Slate. “People will pay even more to stay in a luxury *haunted* hotel. I’ll soon have those spooks hard at work. I’ll make a fortune!”

Within minutes, the ghosts’ tragic tale appeared on the Spirit World Wide Web.

Ghosts’ Online Gazette

SO LONG SHIVERHAM!

HISTORIC HOTEL TO BE FLATTENED
- STAFF FACE SLAVERY TO SLATE

The staff of Shiverham Hall are to become a ‘tourist attraction’ in a new hotel built by Percival Slate.

Percival Slate

It looked as if the ghosts' peaceful life was coming to an end. Next day, the staff watched from the shadows as Slate dreamed of what was to come.

Suddenly, a spooky figure appeared from nowhere.

"Yoo hoo!" she cried.

"Aha!" said Slate. "Another spook, and a very ugly one."

"Don't you recognize me Percy?" said the ghost. "It's me, your Great Aunt Mabel!"

Let Auntie give you a nice big KISS!
Huh?

Slate's ghostly aunt planted a slobbery wet kiss on his cheek. Slate's face turned bright red.

"I read all about you on The Ghosts' Gazette website," said Mabel. "So I've decided to come and live in your lovely new hotel."

"I'll look after you, Percy," cried Mabel. "I'll feed you up on my special cabbage soup and I'll make sure you get a bath and a big kiss every bedtime!"

Slate had been terrified of his aunt when she was alive. Now she was even scarier.

"I've ch..changed my mind," he stammered, tore up his plans, and ran.

All the ghosts cheered. Mr. Quiver approached Great Aunt Mabel and bowed.

"Thank you, madam," he said. "Please stay as our guest for as long as you want – for free."

It was Charlie Crossbones' first day as a pirate.

He'd spent the last ten years at Pirate School. Now he was ready to set sail for treasure.

He knew how to...

read a
treasure map...

unlock a
chest...

...and do lots of other
piratey things.

He even knew how to give a real pirate's laugh.

What's more, Charlie had been lucky enough to inherit his Grandpa's old pirate ship and all the gear to go with it.

But as Charlie looked at his outfit, he realized something was missing. He didn't have a parrot.

Every pirate needs a parrot.

A moment later, Charlie spotted just what he needed.

There were parrots of all shapes and sizes. There was only one problem. They were all too expensive.

As Charlie turned to go, the parrot seller called him back.

"I suppose you could have this one," he said.

Charlie had never seen such a pretty parrot and he was amazed it was so cheap. "You've got a very special bird there!" said the parrot seller.

Now he had his parrot, Charlie wasted no time in setting off on his hunt for treasure.

Out at sea, Charlie spotted a ship named the *Fat Flounder*. He knew it belonged to a rich sailor named Captain Silverside. "I bet that ship is loaded with cash," said Charlie, happily.

Charlie waited until the sailors had gone to lunch. Then he rowed across to the ship and sneaked in through an open window.

Charlie was in luck. He'd climbed into the cabin where the captain kept his treasure.

But he had only just begun to stuff his pockets with gold coins, when disaster struck.

"Sssh!" Charlie hissed at his parrot. But it was too late.

Charlie took one look at Captain Silverside and ran.

COME BACK HERE,
YOU SNEAKY THIEF!

The captain and his men chased Charlie around the deck six times before the poor pirate escaped to his boat.

As he rowed back to his ship, Charlie turned to his parrot with a face like thunder. "Don't ever do that again, you pesky parrot!" he scolded.

But every time they went to sea, the parrot caused trouble.

Just as Charlie was about to steal someone's treasure, the parrot let out a warning cry.

Each time, Charlie only just managed to escape. Soon, he was a nervous wreck.

Whenever he tried to get rid of the parrot...

...it always found its way back to Charlie's shoulder.

As Charlie was eating his supper one evening, he wondered what he could do.

The Laughing Lobster Inn
Super Deluxe Menu
Scrummy Scampi 7 pennies
Mouthwatering Mussels 6 pennies
Deluxe Menu
Crispy Cod 5 pennies
Fancy Fishcakes 4 pennies
Cheap Menu
Shrimp on toast 2 pennies
Very Cheap Menu
Bread & cheese 1 penny

He had never felt so miserable. Thanks to that pesky parrot he was a useless, practically penniless pirate.

Charlie's long face was making the other customers lose their appetites. The landlord tried to cheer him up.

They were so busy talking, neither of them spotted a thief creeping up to the landlord's cash box.

The thief was just about to swipe all the money, when Charlie's parrot squawked into action.

"What a wonderful bird!" said the landlord. "That thief nearly got away with my cash."

This gave Charlie an idea. Perhaps he could put his parrot to good use after all.

The landlord paid Charlie handsomely for his new burglar alarm...

the parrot enjoyed its new job...

...and Charlie had enough money to buy another bird – a quiet one this time.

On the edge of a gloomy forest, three giants were eating their dinner.

These giants were gigantic. They were eating meat as big as rocks. Their spoons were like shovels and their forks were big enough to dig a garden.

But someone was secretly watching them.

His name was Sam and he was a hunter. "I'm going to have some fun with these giants," he said.

Taking aim, he fired his gun at the fork of the fattest giant.

Sam's gun made the giant jump. He poked the fork into his chin.

"Ow!" he yelled. "Who did that? Just wait until I catch you, whoever you are!"

Sam tried to hide, but he wasn't quick enough. The giant spotted him.

He jumped up and grabbed Sam. "Ha ha! Now you're in trouble, boy!" he roared.

"Unless you help us," he added. "We want the princess from the king's castle. You can get her."

"H-how?" squeaked Sam. He was terrified.

"Oh, we'll show you," the giant said. He laughed.

"Do you think he's up to the job?" said the brown-haired giant.

"There's no one else to help us," said the black-haired giant.

"Then let's go!" said the bald-headed giant.

The giants picked up Sam and took him to the castle.
"Everyone's asleep," they told him. "We put a spell on them. But the dog is still awake. You must shoot him."

They pushed Sam through a tiny window.

The castle dog trotted up to Sam, wagging his tail. He didn't bark once. He was a very friendly dog.

Hello there!
What's your name?

"How could I shoot you?" asked Sam, patting him.

Sam decided he wasn't going to help the giants. "I think I'll explore the castle," he said.

In one room, Sam found the princess. He thought she was beautiful. He gazed at her for a long, long time. Then he tiptoed out.

Next, he found a room with a sword hanging on the wall. There was a golden cup beside the sword, with writing on it.

Drink this and use the magic sword to save the princess, read Sam.

Sam was excited. Perhaps he could save the princess from those horrible giants. He tried a sip of the drink...

Mmm... quite tasty...

Glug, glug...

He drank some more. Soon, he'd finished it.

"Now for the sword!" said Sam. He gave a big tug and felt it move, just a little. He tried again.

This time, it came out in a rush. "Ha ha!" said Sam. "Now to get those giants!"

Downstairs, the giants were knocking at the door.

"Let us in!" they bellowed.

"You're too big and the door's too small," said Sam.

"Never mind that!" yelled the giants. "Open this door now!"

"OK," said Sam and he hid behind the door...

As the giants crawled in, he chopped off their heads. The princess was saved.

But Sam began to worry. The king might not like people using his sword. He could be in big trouble. So he ran away.

Back in the castle, the giants' spell soon wore off. The soldiers woke up. They stared at the dead giants. Could it really be true?

Someone's killed the giants!
The king! The king! Fetch the king!

The castle buzzed with excitement. The giants were dead at last. But who had killed them?

The king saw that his sword had gone, too. It was a mystery.

The princess was happiest of all. She dreamed of the handsome hero who had saved her. "I'll marry him...we'll be so happy!" she sighed.

"But we don't know who he is!" said the king.

"Please find him for me, Daddy," she begged.

So the king built an inn. A sign above the door read: *Anyone who tells his life story may stay here for free.*

A year later, Sam passed by. He went inside and told his tale.

It's the giant killer!
Call the princess!

The king was overjoyed to meet the man who'd killed the giants. His daughter was so excited, she married Sam that very day.

Everyone was invited to the wedding... except giants. None of the other giants would have gone anyway. They were far too scared of Sam.

The tale of the kitchen knight

One day, a young stranger arrived at King Arthur's castle. He had beautiful white hands but his clothes were old and torn.

"I have nowhere to go," he told the king. "Please Sire, may I stay for a year?"

King Arthur liked the look of him, so he agreed. "Sir Kay can take care of you," he said.

Grumpy Sir Kay was in charge of the kitchens. He sneered at the young boy. "Hmph! I shall call you Pretty Hands," he said. "Now, let's see how hard you can work."

Work harder,
Pretty Hands!

Pretty Hands stirred soup...

peeled vegetables...

mopped floors...

and washed dishes.

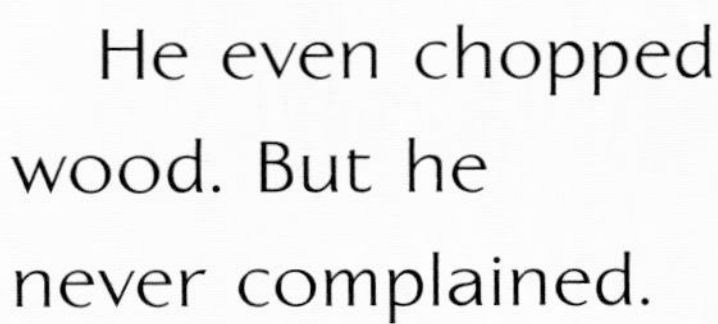

He even chopped wood. But he never complained.

When Pretty Hands had been at the castle for almost a year, a lady came to Camelot. Her name was Linnet and she was very rude.

"Get me a knight! I need help!" she declared. "My sister Lyonesse has been captured by the Red Knight."

The Red Knight!
He's as strong as seven men!

No one wanted to help Linnet. Then Pretty Hands stepped forward. "I'll rescue your sister," he announced.

Everyone was shocked. He was only the kitchen boy.

Lady Linnet was furious. "I want a real knight," she stormed, "not a boy who smells of the kitchen!"

"Don't worry, my Lady," said King Arthur. "Sir Lancelot will make him into a real knight first."

Just before he was knighted, Pretty Hands told Sir Lancelot a secret. His real name was Gareth and he was Sir Gawain's brother.

The next day, Sir Gareth set off with Lady Linnet to rescue her sister. They faced dragons and worse. Gareth killed them all, but Linnet wasn't impressed.

At last, they reached the Red Knight's castle. Lady Lyonesse was locked in a tower. When she saw Sir Gareth she smiled. Gareth took one look at her and fell in love.

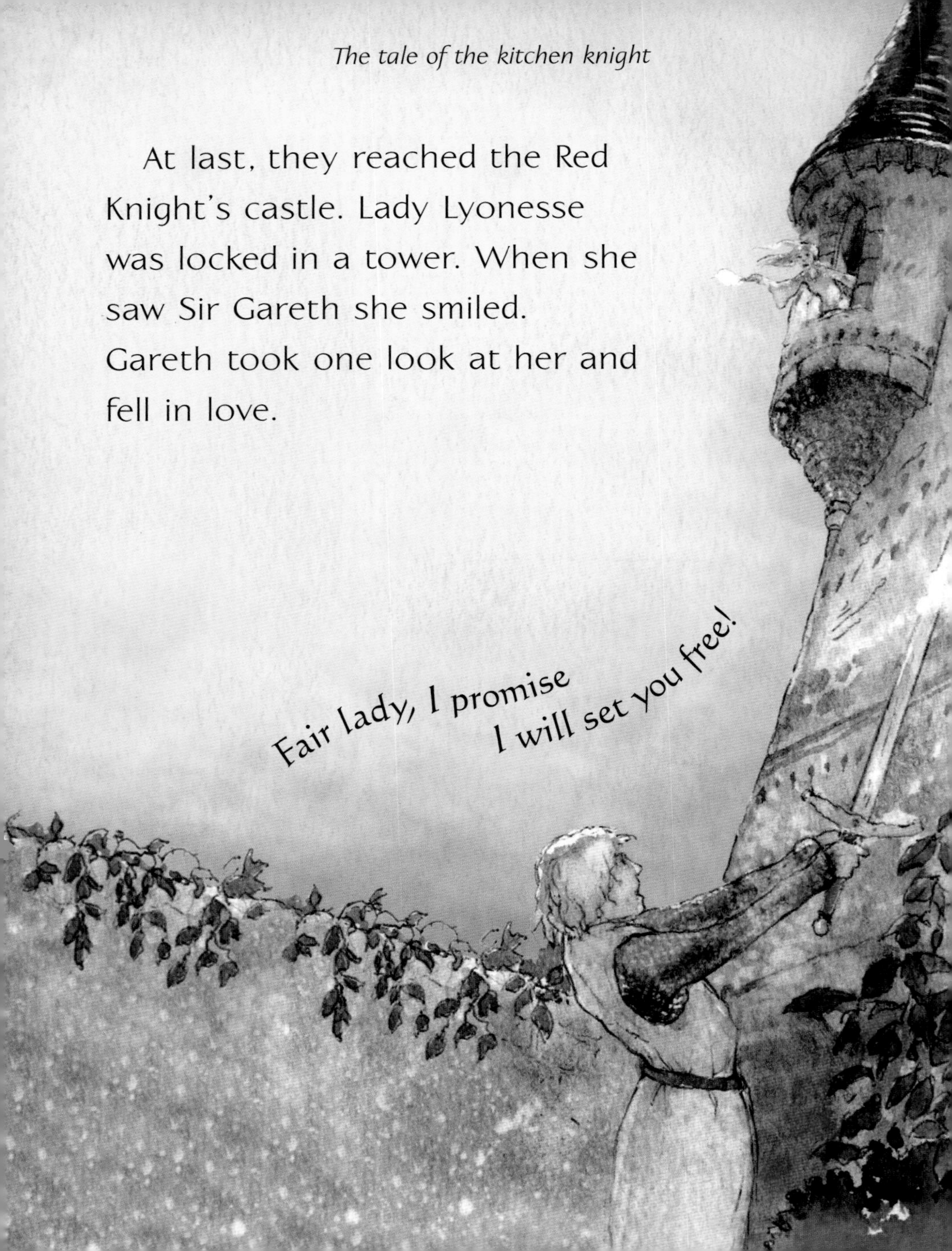
Fair lady, I promise
I will set you free!

Gareth rode up to the castle and hammered on the door. There was a terrible roar. Then the door opened and the Red Knight thundered out.

I'll tear you to pieces!
Just you try!

Sir Gareth and the Red Knight fought for hours. It was a hard battle and both of them were badly wounded. But, as the sun sank and the stars rose, Sir Gareth finally won.

Leaving the Red Knight on the ground, Gareth raced to the tower and unlocked Lady Lyonesse. Before she could say a word, he asked her to marry him.

Oh, yes!

Will you be my wife?

Back at Camelot, King Arthur gave the couple a grand wedding. When Gareth told him his real name, he was welcomed to the Round Table to sit beside his brother.

"Not bad – for a kitchen boy!" said Lady Linnet.

Attack of the swamp monster

Tom Smudge loved to listen to his Grandpa Jess tell creepy stories about the old days.

"Did I ever tell you about the swamp monster?" asked the old man one afternoon.

"No," gulped Tom nervously.

"It happened years ago," began Grandpa Jess. "I was a farmhand on Roy's ranch, when one of the cows went missing."

"I searched all day with no luck. As night fell, I spotted a muddy trail leading to the middle of the swamp..."

"What happened next?" asked Tom, with a shiver.

"A terrible, slithering sound filled the air, and I found myself face to face with a horrible, hideous..."

Mrs. Smudge suddenly burst into the room waving a piece of paper at Tom.

"I need you to go to the store and get these things!" she said.

"Can't I hear the end of Grandpa's story first?" begged Tom.

Grocery list
Soap for Grandpa
2 large bottles of bubble bath
Lots of broccoli
Small cabbage
Peas

"No. Now, off you go," said Mrs. Smudge. "And hurry back," she added. "You haven't had a bath yet."

Tom groaned. He hated baths.

He was trudging back from the store when his friends asked him to play football. Thinking of the waiting bath, Tom quickly agreed.

By the time the game ended, it was almost dark. Tom decided to take a shortcut home across the swamp.

He'd only been walking for a minute, when he heard a sinister, squelching sound. Green stalks seemed to be curling around him.

These weeds are
very thick!

But they weren't weeds that Tom could feel tightening around his ankles...

Dinner time!

Aaaaargh!
The swamp monster!
Heeeelp!

Tom struggled in the slimy creature's grasp. The more he squirmed, the tighter the monster squeezed.

Tom wished he'd never stopped to play football.

The monster dragged him closer to its huge, slimy, smelly mouth.

Suddenly there was a crack. The monster had smashed the bottles in Tom's bag.

In seconds, the murky swamp water became a mass of sweet-smelling bubbles.

The monster choked and spluttered on the foamy water. Tom slipped from its grasp. They were both getting the bath of their lives.

By now, several people had heard Tom's shouts and come to help. They took one look at the new, squeaky-clean monster and burst out laughing.

The monster was so embarrassed, it swam off and was never seen again.

As for Tom, he had the best reward ever. He didn't need a bath for a week.

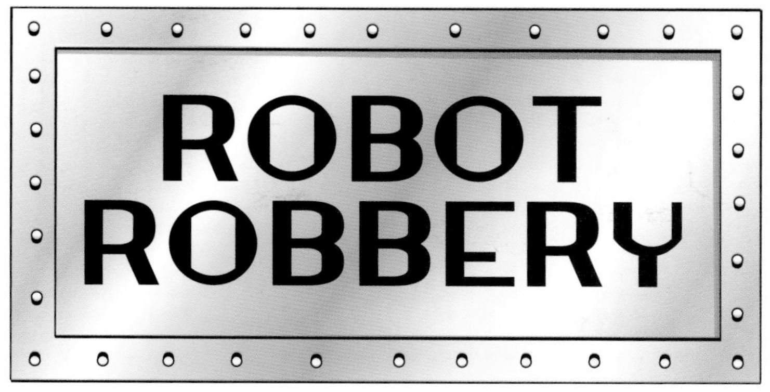

Jay C. B. was the hardest-working robot on the building site. He had ten different tools, so he was always digging and drilling.

But Jay liked the end of each day best. Only then could he switch off and recharge his battery.

One night, as Jay was recharging, someone broke in and carried him off.

When Jay was fully charged, he awoke to find himself in a strange workshop. A wild-haired man was fiddling with Jay's control panel. "Hey, what's going on?" he gulped.

Quiet, you
tin-plated twit!

"Who are you?" cried Jay, "and what do you want?"

"The name's Filch," snapped the man. "The rest you'll find out soon enough."

"But I should be digging back at the site," cried Jay.

"I have a much better job for you," said Filch. "I want you to dig for me... into Bullion's Bank!"

I'm not taking
orders from you!

"When I've reprogramed you, you'll do whatever I want," snarled the crook.

Later that day, Filch ordered Jay to follow him to the bank.

"No!" said Jay.

Filch pushed a button on a remote control. Jay followed.

Okay, metal muscles
- start digging!

But Jay refused to dig. Filch angrily flicked two switches on his remote control.

"I obey!" said Jay, and began burrowing into the ground at top speed.

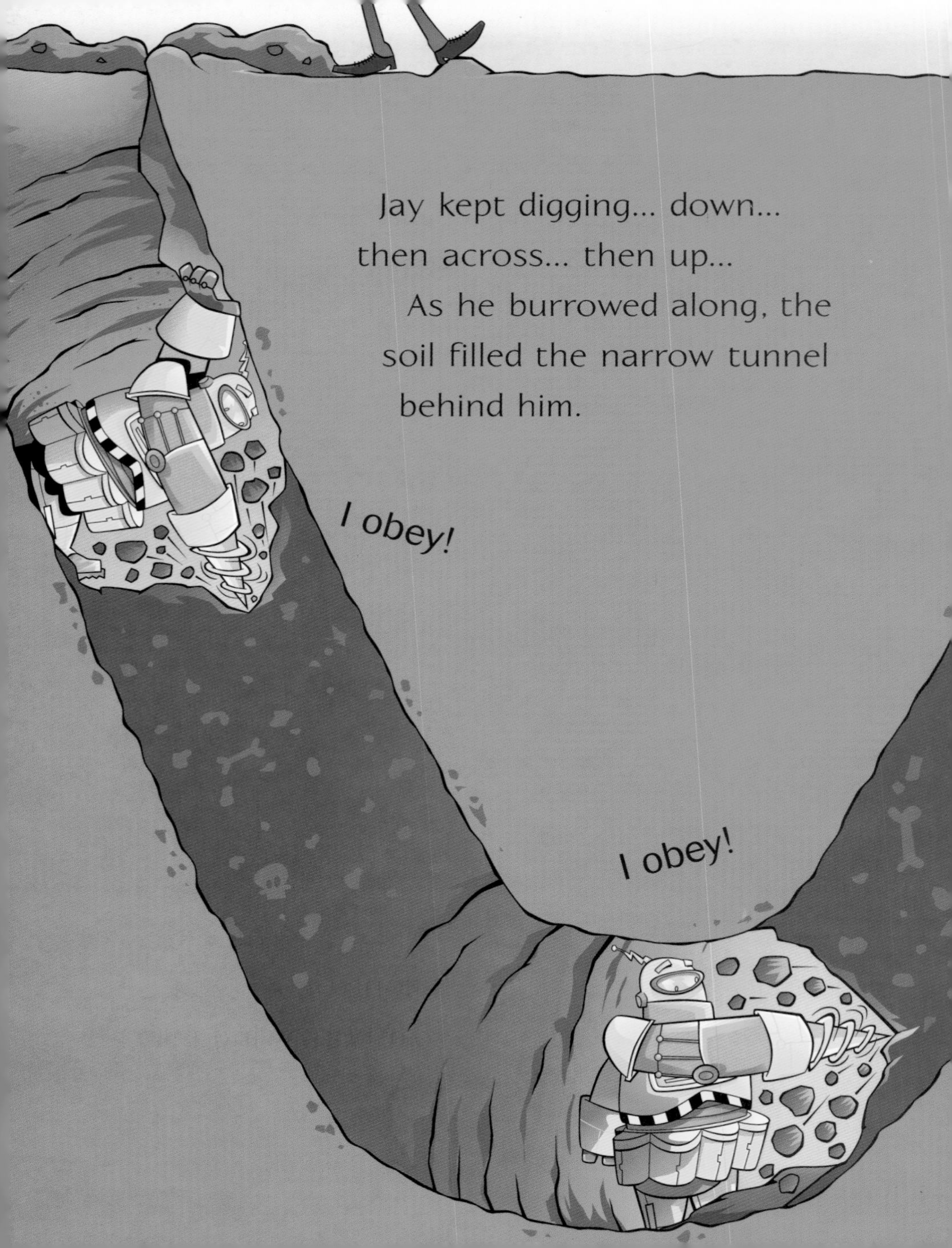

Jay kept digging... down... then across... then up...

As he burrowed along, the soil filled the narrow tunnel behind him.

Soon Jay emerged in Bullion's Bank. Outside, Filch watched Jay's progress on a tiny screen. He twisted a dial and Jay drilled through a thick metal door.

Filch was delighted. "Only the electric inner door left to go," he said with a grin. "Then all the bank's gold will be mine!"

Jay's saw buzzed into action. But as it sliced through the door, an electric shock blasted Jay off his feet.

Suddenly, Jay felt different. He could switch off his saw.

"I'm free!" he cried. "That electric shock must have stopped Filch's program."

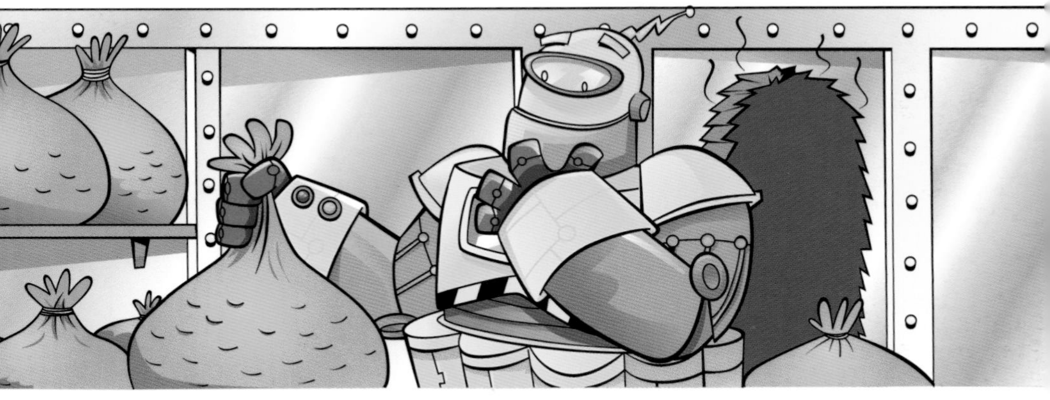

"Now I'll fix that no-good crook," thought Jay.

Minutes later, Jay popped out of the tunnel and handed Filch two big sacks.

"Run!" he cried. "The guards saw me stealing the gold."

Filch ran home as fast as he could. But he was in for a surprise.

The greedy crook excitedly tipped out the contents of the sacks, only to to find...

Jay had filled the sacks with rubble from the tunnel.

Filch spat out a mouthful of dirt. "That's the last time I trust a robot!" he shouted.

Treasure Island

This is the story of my incredible adventure on Treasure Island. I'm Jim Hawkins and I help my mother run the Admiral Benbow Inn...

Each day was just like the last, until the morning a stranger arrived.

I was sweeping, when an old sea captain strode up the road, singing. He saw me and stopped outside the inn.

"Many people here?" he growled. I shook my head. "Then I'll stay," said the captain.

Can you
do something
for me?

"Name's Billy Bones," he told me, giving me a silver coin. "Look out for a sailor with one leg," he whispered, "and I'll give you a coin every month."

During the day, Billy Bones strode along the cliffs peering at the sea through his telescope. At night, he told scary stories about pirates. He stayed for months, but he never paid my mother a penny.

And old Captain
Scar stood alone on
the deck with his jagged
cutlass in his hand...

One frosty morning, when Billy Bones was out, a man came to the inn.

"Is there a captain staying here?" he asked. Just then, Bones strode through the door. "Hello Bill," said the man. Bones looked as though he had seen a ghost.

"Black Dog!" gasped Bones.

"Yes," sneered the man, "and I've come for what's hidden in that sea chest of yours."

You'll never get your hands on it, you interfering devil!

With a clang of steel, both men drew their swords. Bones struck Black Dog on the shoulder and chased him out of the inn.

Bones was so shocked that he grew sick and had to stay in bed. "You've got to help me Jim," he begged. "Black Dog sailed with a pirate named Captain Flint. Now his whole crew will be after me. If you ever see strange men hanging around, get help!"

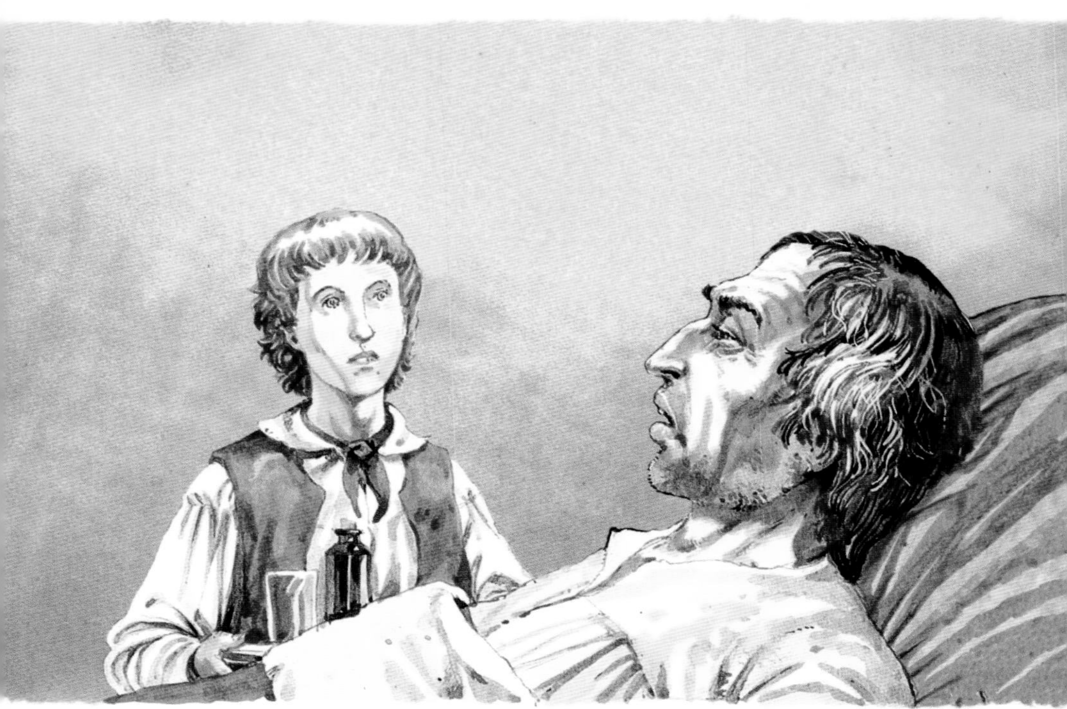

Only a few days later, I heard an odd noise outside. Tap... tap... tap... A blind man was trudging along, tapping the road with his stick.

"Where am I?" he asked.

"The Admiral Benbow Inn," I replied.

The man grabbed my arm with an icy hand. "Take me to Billy Bones," he hissed.

When Bones saw the blind man, he was horrified. The man gave Bones a note and hurried away.

With trembling fingers, Bones read the message. "The pirates!" he gasped. "They're coming tonight!" With a cry of pain, he fell to the floor. To my horror, he was dead.

I didn't like the sound of those pirates at all. But Mother was determined to see what Bones had hidden in his chest. So, that night, I locked all the doors and windows of the inn and we went to the captain's room.

His chest was full of old clothes and weapons, but at the very bottom we found papers and a bag of gold.

Excitedly, we began to count the money. Just then, someone rattled the door of the inn. Then I heard a faint tapping. Tap... tap... tap...

We grabbed the money and papers and ran out into the night. I'd only just pulled my mother into a hiding place when a gang of men rushed to the inn.

They smashed down the door and stormed through our home, shouting, "Bones is dead! Find the papers!"

Suddenly the blind man threw open a window.

"The papers have gone!" he shrieked. "Find the boy!"

But as the pirates came closer to our hiding place, a group of soldiers galloped over the hill.

The pirates fled.

"We heard you were in danger," the captain of the soldiers said to me. "Sorry we took so long."

"The pirates wanted these papers," I explained. "I think we should take them to the Hall and show Squire Trelawny."

Where did you get them?
We found them in Billy Bones' chest.

Squire Trelawny was having dinner with his friend Dr. Livesey. They were amazed by my story.

When Dr. Livesey opened the packet of papers, he found a map.

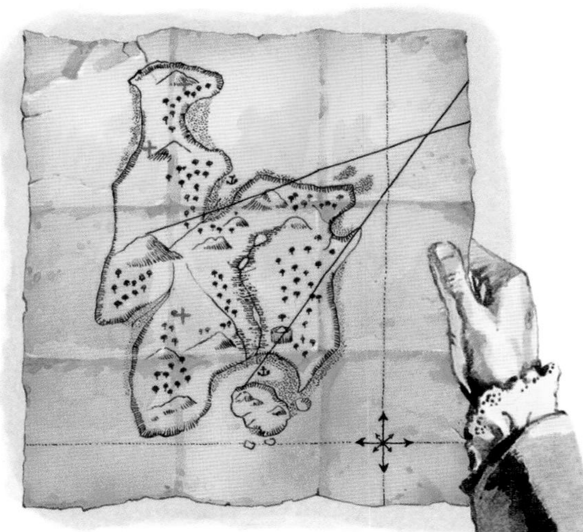

"No wonder Flint's pirates wanted this," he said. "It shows where his treasure is buried!"

Squire Trelawny was thrilled. “Here’s my plan,” he said. “We shall sail to that island and find Flint’s treasure. And you, Jim, can come with us!”

But don’t tell anyone
about the treasure!

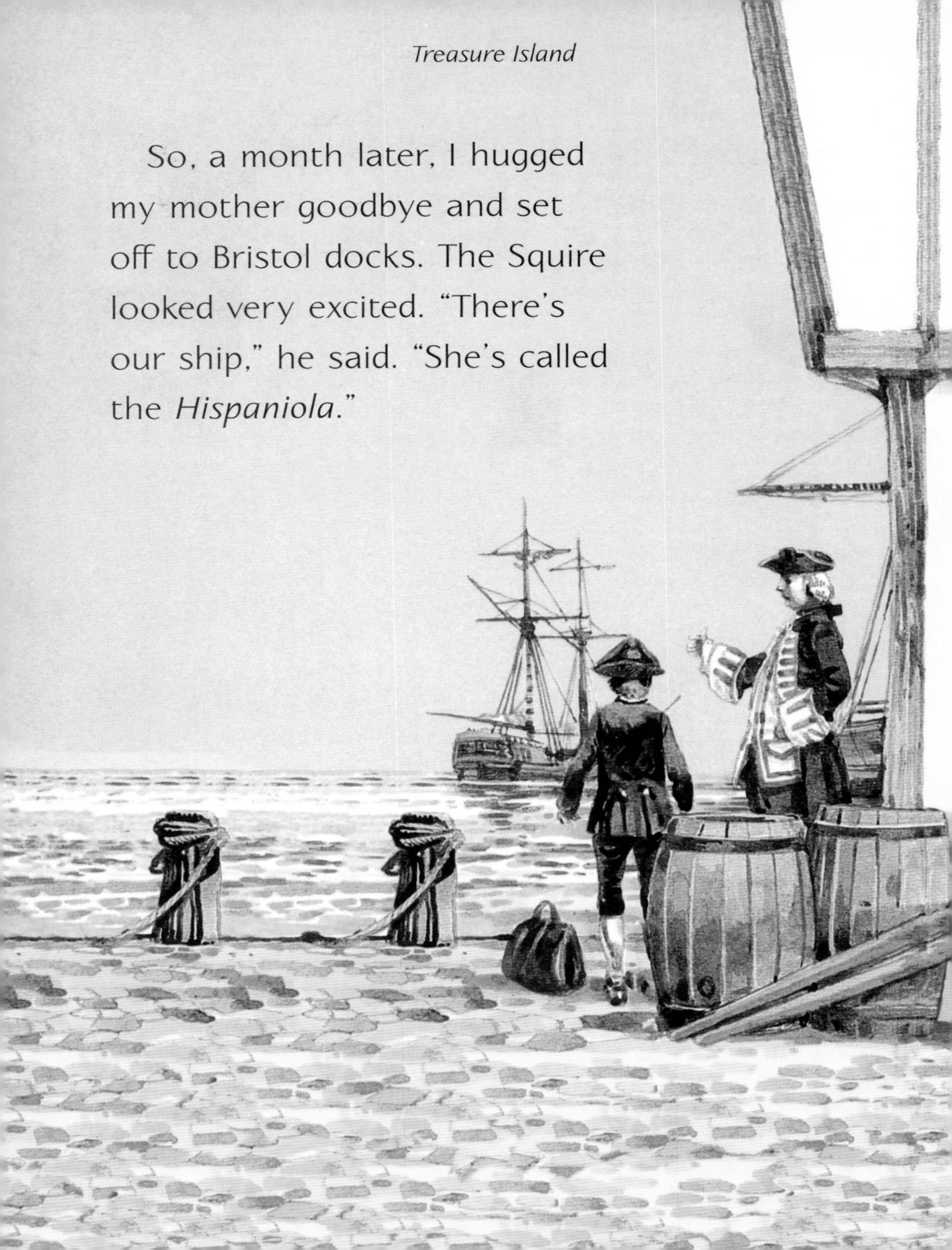

So, a month later, I hugged my mother goodbye and set off to Bristol docks. The Squire looked very excited. "There's our ship," he said. "She's called the *Hispaniola*."

He asked me to take a message to the ship's cook, Long John Silver. I was horrified to see he had only one leg. Was this the sailor Bones had paid me to watch out for? He seemed friendly enough.

Besides, I had something else to worry about.

Captain Smollett, who was in charge of the *Hispaniola*, was angry. “I thought this voyage was a secret,” he snapped, “but it seems the whole crew knows you’re after Flint’s treasure. I don’t trust them.”

Those sailors are a
shifty-looking bunch,
if you ask me!

We were all worried by the captain's news, but it was too late to find a new crew. The next morning, we set sail.

Pieces of eight! Lovely boy!

During the voyage, I made friends with Long John. I liked the talking parrot who sat on his shoulder.

But one night, I was climbing into a barrel to get an apple...

Sounds good! What's the plan?

...when I overheard Long John whispering to a young sailor. "I was Captain Flint's second-in-command," he said. "Join us pirates and get rich."

I broke out in a sweat. Captain Smollett was right. Some of the men were pirates.

"We'll wait until we have the treasure," continued Long John, "then we'll kill the captain and his friends."

"Oh no!" I thought. "I've got to tell the others."

Just then there was a cry of "Land ahoy!" Everyone rushed onto the deck to look at Treasure Island.

I ran to the captain's cabin and told everyone what I'd heard.

"We can't give up now!" said the captain. "We must find out who's on our side and be ready to fight."

Next morning, we arrived at the island. The men wanted to lie on the beach. Instead, they had to mend sails and scrub the decks. The sailors started grumbling.

Captain Smollett, scared they'd rebel, gave them the afternoon off.

The sailors eagerly rowed for the shore. I was desperate to go too, so I slipped into one of the boats.

When we reached the beach, I jumped out and ran off into the trees. I couldn't wait to have a look around the island.

I was exploring the island when I heard Long John Silver talking to one of the sailors.

Join us pirates or
you'll pay the price!

The sailor turned and ran. With a growl, Long John hurled his walking stick, knocking the man down and killing him.

He KILLED him!

I ran away into the forest, stumbling and gasping.

But then I saw a shadowy figure dodge behind a tree. As I drew closer, a wild man sprang out!

Don't hurt me!
I'm only poor Ben Gunn.

"My pirate friends left me here to die," said Ben. "Please help me escape from the island. I'll make you rich if you do."

Just at that moment, the distant boom of a cannon shook the air. "I must go and help my friends!" I thought.

Meanwhile, as I found out later, Dr. Livesey was searching for me with one of the sailors. They came across a fort made of logs on a hill.

Suddenly, they heard a piercing scream from the ship. "The pirates are attacking," said the doctor. "Quick! We'll get the others and hide here."

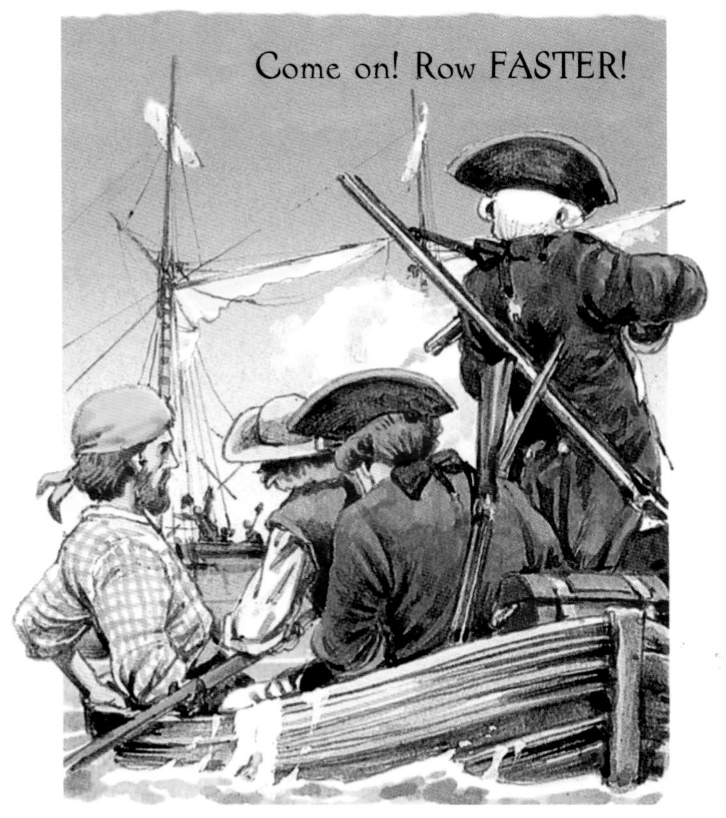

The pair rushed back to the ship, helped the captain load a boat with guns and rowed desperately for the shore. Some pirates fired at them with the ship's cannon, but they reached the land safely.

So, as I ran across the island, I saw the captain's flag fluttering over the log fort. I scrambled over the fence and dashed inside.

"I've just seen Long John Silver kill a sailor!" I cried, panting. "And, when I ran away, I met a man called Ben Gunn in the woods!"

"Silver killed a sailor?" said the Squire, looking worried.

"We don't have many guns," added Dr. Livesey, "and the pirates are fierce fighters."

We stayed up all night, trying to decide what to do. But, as the sun came up, we still didn't have a plan.

At dawn, Long John Silver came hobbling up the hill. "Give us the treasure map," he said, "and we won't harm you."

"We don't bargain with pirates," said the captain.

"Then you're all dead men," sneered Long John and walked off.

The captain looked at us.

"Get ready to fight, my lads," he said. Time seemed to stop. It became very hot and quiet.

Suddenly, shots rang out and pirates swarmed over the fence. The captain's men opened fire and a savage battle began.

Finally, the fighting was over and the last few pirates ran off, defeated. Dr. Livesey took the treasure map and disappeared into the woods.

I guessed he had gone to find Ben Gunn and I wanted to help. Taking two pistols, I crept away to join him.

But, as I walked along the beach, I found a boat Ben Gunn had made. It gave me a wonderful idea. I would cut the *Hispaniola* loose from its rope. With luck, the few pirates left on board would be taken by surprise and the ship would run aground! "I'll give those pirates something to think about," I thought.

It was easy to launch the little boat into the waves, but it wasn't so easy to steer it. When I tried to paddle, the boat just spun in circles.

Luckily, the tide swept me over to the ship. Catching hold of the anchor rope, I sliced through it.

I could hear people shouting inside, so I quietly crawled up to a window. Two pirates were locked in a vicious fight.

The ship moved suddenly, startling the pirates. I dived back into my boat and crouched at the bottom. I hid, with my eyes shut, as the waves carried me out to sea.

Hours later, I woke with my head spinning. It was already daytime and I was bobbing on the sea not far from the island. But, when I tried to paddle ashore, the boat was caught by a huge wave and plunged underwater for a second.

I was terrified. I realized I had no control over the boat and feared I'd be lost at sea forever. Then, to my great relief, I saw the *Hispaniola* drifting my way. There was only one thing to do. I would have to get on board and try to take charge.

All of a sudden, the ship reared up on the sea and towered over me. I sprang up and managed to catch hold of it, just as it smashed the little boat to tiny pieces.

Holding on with all my strength, I clambered along a mast as the ship rocked and plunged.

Gently, I swung myself down onto the deck. The whole place seemed strangely quiet.

In a corner, two pirates were lying in a pool of blood. One was dead, but the other groaned and looked up. It was Israel Hands, one of Long John Silver's friends.

What are you doing here?
I've come to take the ship back to Captain Smollett!

Hands smiled slyly. "I'll help you sail the ship to the island if you like," he offered.

But as we approached a bay, I heard a noise behind me. I whirled around. Hands was clutching a dagger, ready to strike.

What are you doing?
Getting the ship back!

He lunged at me, but I skipped to one side. Then I tried to fire one of the pistols... There was only a dull click.

In desperation, I scrambled up the mast ropes, climbing higher and higher.

You can't escape that easily, lad!

At one point I glanced down. Hands was climbing after me! I paused to reload my pistols.

Suddenly, Hands hurled his dagger, striking me on the shoulder. I have never felt such pain, before or since.

As I shouted out, both pistols went off. Hands screamed and dropped into the sea.

With a thumping heart and throbbing shoulder, I climbed down and swam ashore. I'd escaped. And now the *Hispaniola* was ready for the captain. Eagerly, I set off across the island to find my friends.

When I finally reached the log fort, it was dark. I crept inside, stumbling in the gloom.

Suddenly, a weird voice shrieked, "Pieces of eight!" It was the parrot. I tried to run, but someone grabbed me and held up a light.

To my dismay, I was surrounded by pirates! "Your friends have gone," Long John said. "There's only us now." Another pirate snarled and lunged at me with a knife. "Hey!" growled Long John, "I'm in charge here."

The pirates glared at him. "We want a new leader," one of them said. Long John took something out of his pocket and held it up.

Everyone gasped: Flint's treasure map! I was puzzled, but Long John wouldn't tell me how it came into his hands.

THREE CHEERS FOR OLD SILVER!

Next morning, to my surprise, Dr. Livesey arrived. He'd agreed to look after the wounded pirates.

Long John was determined to keep me a prisoner, but he let me talk to the doctor for a while.

"I thought you'd gone," I said, telling Dr. Livesey about my adventure on the *Hispaniola*.

Well done, Jim!
Don't worry,
we'll rescue you.

Soon after breakfast, the pirates set off to find the treasure. They took me with them.

"However will I escape?" I thought in a panic.

The map said Flint's chest was buried under a tall tree in the shadow of Spyglass Hill.

As we neared the spot marked "X" on the map, a pirate up ahead began to shout. But he hadn't found treasure... He'd found a skeleton.

In the silence that followed, a spine-chilling voice filled the air. It sang a sailor's song. "The ghost of Captain Flint!" cried the pirates.

Flint is coming to get us! RUN!

"Don't be stupid," said Long John. "It's just someone trying to scare us."

Another pirate spotted a tall tree and everyone charged over to it. But at the bottom of the tree was an empty hole. The treasure had gone.

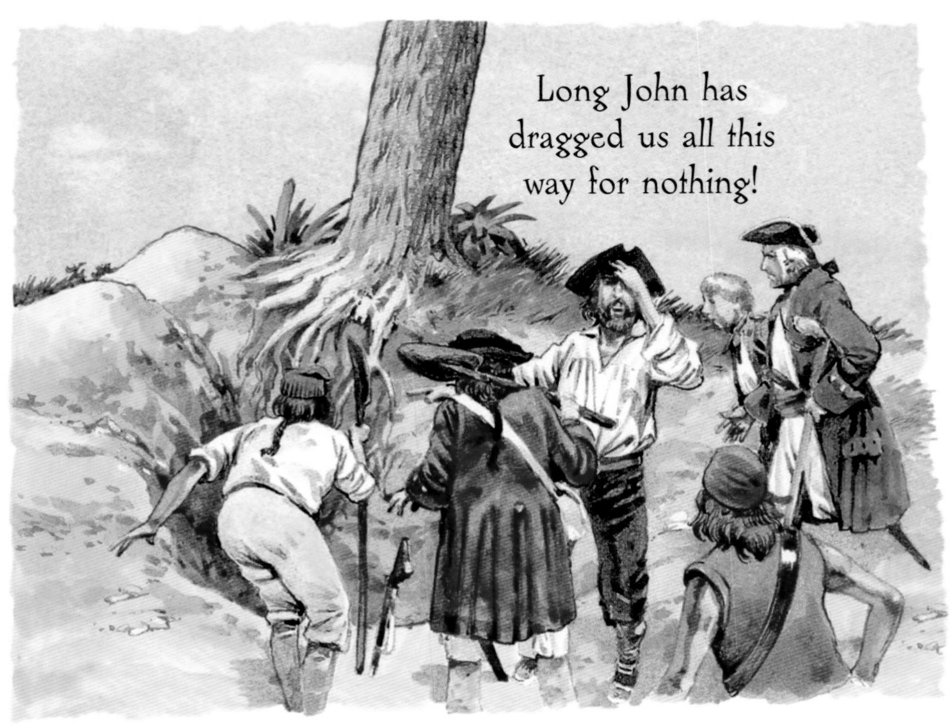

Long John has
dragged us all this
way for nothing!

Long John tapped me on my good shoulder. "There's going to be trouble," he whispered. Was he on our side now?

I clutched my pistols tightly, feeling sweat run down my neck.

The men are
going to be furious.
Get ready to fight!

The pirates stared at Long John menacingly and drew their guns. Just then, shots rang out. Dr. Livesey and Ben Gunn charged out of the bushes with a sailor named Gray. The terrified pirates ran off.

"Quick!" said the doctor. "We must get to the boats before the pirates." We sprinted to the beach, with Long John hobbling behind.

"Don't leave me!" he panted. "The others will kill me."

I'll damage this boat,
so the pirates can't follow us!

We clambered aboard a boat and rowed for the *Hispaniola*.

As Gray rowed, Dr. Livesey cleared up a mystery. "I tricked Silver with the treasure map," he told me. "I wanted to distract the pirates. I knew Ben had found Flint's treasure years ago."

Leaving Gray behind to guard the *Hispaniola*, the rest of us headed for Ben's cave and the treasure.

The Squire and
Captain Smollett
are waiting for
us in Ben's cave.

Ben's cave was enormous. The ground was covered in huge heaps of glittering coins, gold bars and jewels that gleamed in the firelight.

The Squire and Captain Smollett were thrilled to see me. That night, we had a grand feast to celebrate finding Flint's treasure.

Next morning, we loaded up the ship with the treasure and sailed away. We took Long John along, but during the voyage, Ben Gunn helped him escape with some gold.

"I thought we'd be better off without him," Ben said.

When we landed at Bristol docks, I hugged everyone goodbye and took my share of the gold. I never saw Long John Silver again.

I never did go back to Treasure Island, but sometimes, in my dreams, I hear the waves on the sand or Long John's parrot squawking, "Pieces of Eight!"

1001 Nights

The story of Sinbad the Sailor comes from a collection of Arabic folk tales called *The Book of One Thousand and One Nights*. In this book, a girl named Scheherazade marries a king who threatens to chop off her head. She tells him a tale each night that ends with a cliffhanger. Because the king wants to know the ending to each story, he spares her life again and again. Eventually he gives in and lets her live.

Arthurian legends

Sir Gawain and the Green Knight and *The tale of the kitchen knight* are both set in the legendary court of King Arthur. Arthur may or may not have existed, but legends about the king have been popular ever since medieval times. Stories tell that King Arthur ruled over all of England, with his beautiful wife Guinevere by his side and a band of brave knights at his command. He was advised by a wise and mysterious old wizard named Merlin.

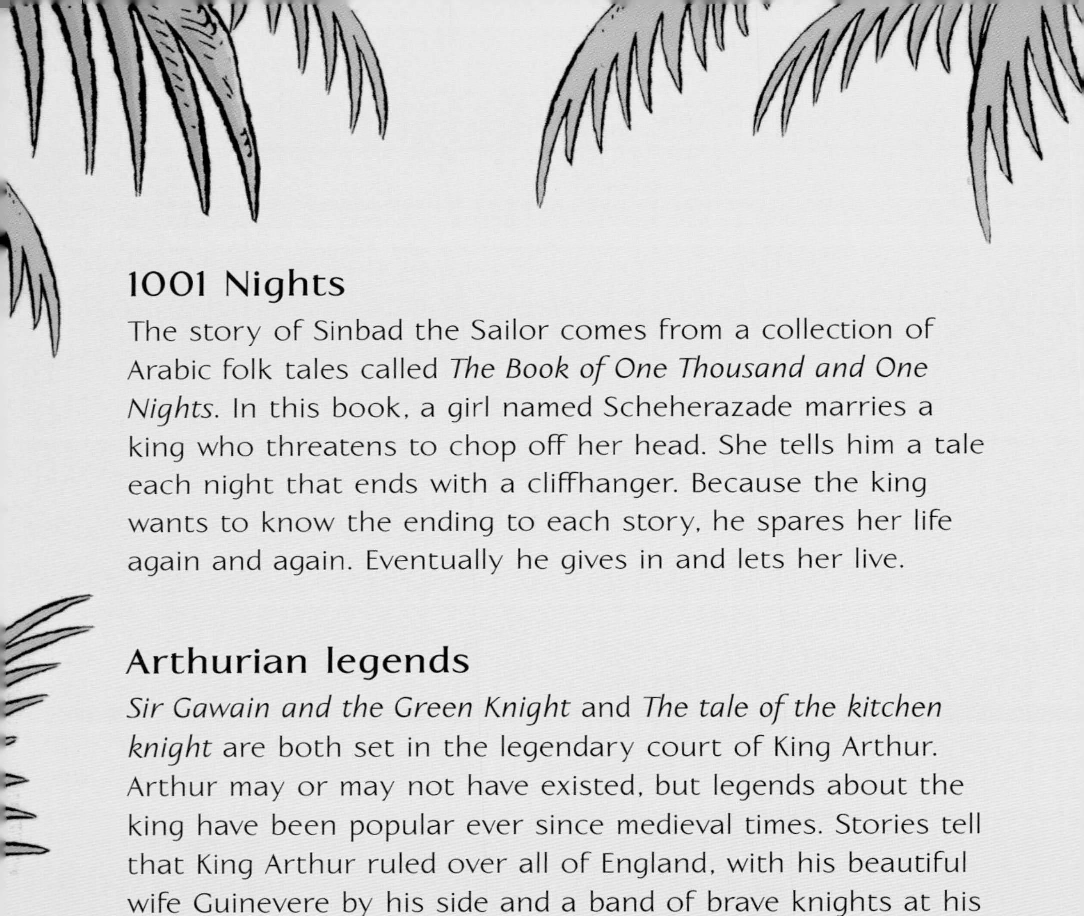

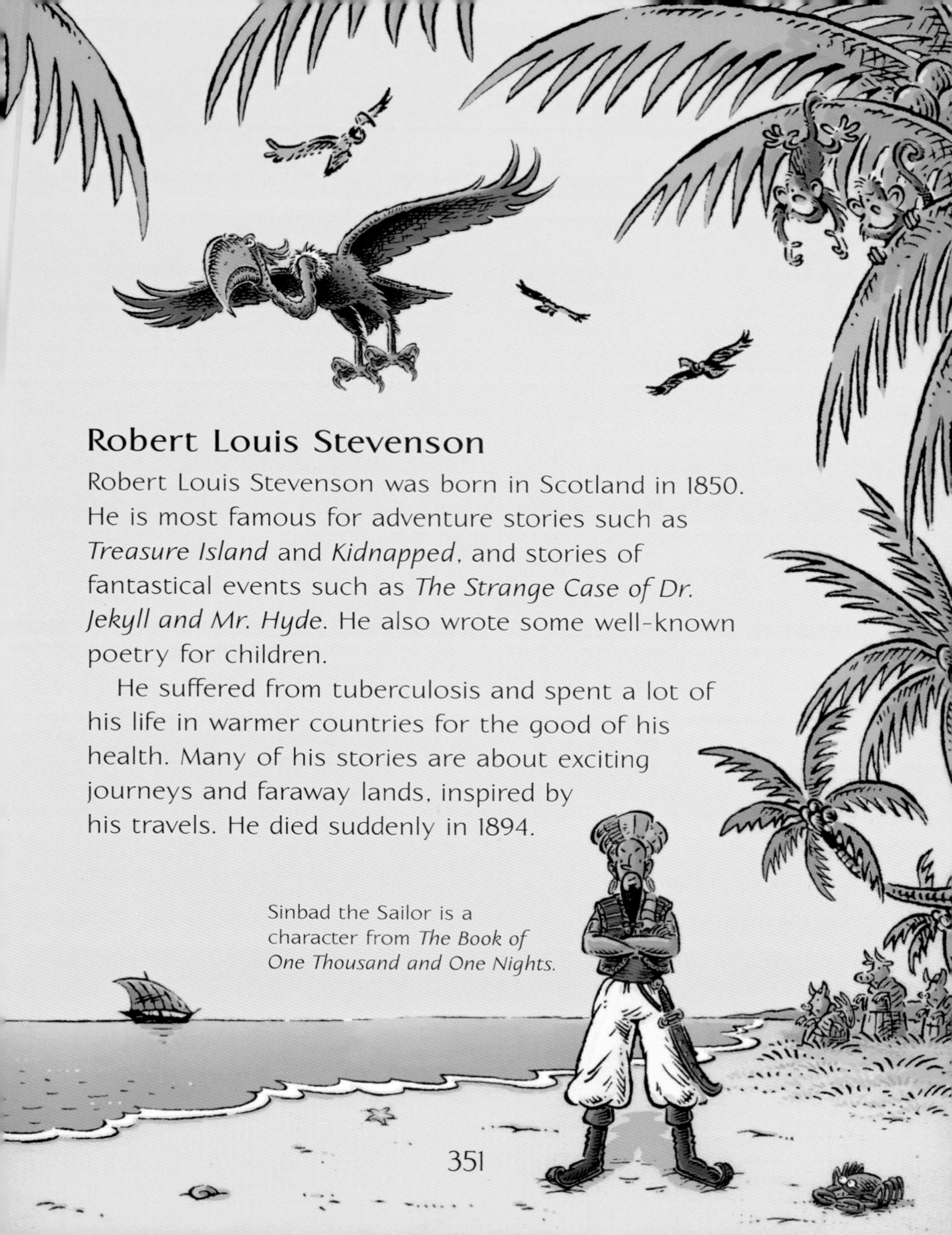

Robert Louis Stevenson

Robert Louis Stevenson was born in Scotland in 1850. He is most famous for adventure stories such as *Treasure Island* and *Kidnapped*, and stories of fantastical events such as *The Strange Case of Dr. Jekyll and Mr. Hyde*. He also wrote some well-known poetry for children.

He suffered from tuberculosis and spent a lot of his life in warmer countries for the good of his health. Many of his stories are about exciting journeys and faraway lands, inspired by his travels. He died suddenly in 1894.

Sinbad the Sailor is a character from *The Book of One Thousand and One Nights.*

Digital manipulation by Tom Lalonde
and Mike Wheatley

First published in 2006 by Usborne Publishing Ltd., Usborne House, 83-85 Saffron Hill, London ECIN 8RT, England. www.usborne.com

Printed in China. UE. First published in America in 2007.